Christian G. Sullivan is a writer who resides just outside of Detroit, Michigan. He grew up in a large family of nine. Although a private person, he realized that the Creator has given him a gift to write and create. While in college, after becoming friends with the school newspaper editor, Sullivan was convinced that he wanted to be a writer. He received rave reviews from his peers, which enhanced his confidence to pursue his dream. Sullivan wants his works to be his legacy. His inspiration is to do more than humanitarian work, with hope that he will help others.

I would like to dedicate this book to my parents.

Christian Sullivan

THE RIVERSIDE STALKERS

AUSTIN MACAULEY PUBLISHERS™
LONDON · CAMBRIDGE · NEW YORK · SHARJAH

Copyright © Christian Sullivan 2023

All rights reserved. No part of this publication may be reproduced, distributed, or transmitted in any form or by any means, including photocopying, recording, or other electronic or mechanical methods, without the prior written permission of the publisher, except in the case of brief quotations embodied in critical reviews and certain other noncommercial uses permitted by copyright law. For permission requests, write to the publisher.

Any person who commits any unauthorized act in relation to this publication may be liable to criminal prosecution and civil claims for damages.

This is a work of fiction. Names, characters, businesses, places, events, locales, and incidents are either the products of the author's imagination or used in a fictitious manner. Any resemblance to actual persons, living or dead, or actual events is purely coincidental.

Ordering Information
Quantity sales: Special discounts are available on quantity purchases by corporations, associations, and others. For details, contact the publisher at the address below.

Publisher's Cataloging-in-Publication data
Sullivan, Christian
The Riverside Stalkers

ISBN 9781645759003 (Paperback)
ISBN 9781645758990 (Hardback)
ISBN 9781645759010 (ePub e-book)

Library of Congress Control Number: 2023905830

www.austinmacauley.com/us

First Published 2023
Austin Macauley Publishers LLC
40 Wall Street, 33rd Floor, Suite 3302
New York, NY 10005
USA

mail-usa@austinmacauley.com
+1 (646) 5125767

My wife, Karen Sullivan

A small town of about 10,000 people who reside in the southwestern part of Pennsylvania, lives a ruthless mean and evil man who rules the town and all of the people. Can six teenagers answer the cries of the town's people, and free them from evil and despair? Brace yourself, for this action-packed heart filled story of what vampirism can accomplish.

Chapter 1

"Yes, sir, what can I do for you, Mr. Mendoza?"

"I came to collect what is due to me every month, you know the rules."

"Excuse me, this is my boy Jeremy, Mr. Mendoza."

"Jeremy, little Jeremy, my, my, he is growing."

"Yes, he is, sir. He is sixteen now. He is a good boy."

"Good, that is how he supposed to be, a good boy."

"Jeremy, when you get older, you are going to owe me like your pa here. So where is my money?"

"I had to buy a new pair of eyeglasses for my youngest, Mr. Mendoza. I'm not going to have the usual amount of money that I give you."

"So, are you telling me that you are going short me little guy?"

"No, I'm not saying that at all, I will have a little more money next month and can catch up then."

"Why you take this." Mr. Mendoza punches Jeremy's dad, he falls to the floor.

"No, no, no, Mr. Mendoza, my nose is bleeding don't hit me anymore in front of my boy. Please, please Mr. Mendoza, stop hitting me please."

"Leave my dad alone, leave him alone, stop it stop it!"

"Well, now you see what will happen when I don't get paid you better remember it, boy!"

"Stop, Mr. Mendoza, I will pay you your money next month."

"Now leave! Leave us alone."

"Dad, dad, are you alright? You are bleeding from the mouth."

"I will be alright, don't worry, son."

"Mr. Mendoza didn't have to beat you up. This is an evil man. I hate him I hate him so much."

"Someday, I'm going to kill him."

"Forget about him, son. He weighs over 200 lbs. and he also got a lot of men that work for him that don't mind doing harm. He can hurt you, son, so just pretend you never saw this. I will be fine. I never taught you about the evil in this world. Mother and I tried to shield you from the bad world, Jeremy."

"You have been a good father. You didn't do anything wrong, Dad."

"I got my new job at Mr. Mendoza water plant which meant everybody had to pay a big fee to him son."

"Why, Dad? Why does everyone have to pay Mr. Mendoza?"

"Jeremy, Mr. Mendoza owns everything in town. All the citizens in town also have to pay him a tax fee."

"Really, Dad, this isn't right."

"No, Jeremy, it isn't right, but we can't do anything about it."

Chapter 2

"Hello, Tara."

"Hi, Mom, have you been expecting me?"

"No, I was not expecting you to come by today."

"Well, I'm here." Mr. Mendoza's quest is to make his rounds to all the town's people to collect his money. He arrives at Tara's house. "Who is this pretty girl?"

"She is my daughter, Mr. Mendoza."

"She's a mighty pretty girl, beautiful girl."

"She got a boyfriend?"

"Huh?" Right at that time, Tara had a disturbing look on her face.

"Why are you asking, Mr. Mendoza?"

"Just asking she's too pretty to be wasted."

"Look, Mr. Mendoza, whatever's gotten into your head, get it out, my daughter's off limits; she's only sixteen years old."

"Hey, girl, what's your name?"

"Don't tell him, you're here to see me, leave my daughter alone."

"My name is Tara, and I'm not afraid of you."

"I'll remember that this girl got guts, Bertha."

"Why are you here, Mr. Mendoza? I paid my dues to you."

"Yeah, you did, Bertha, but your taxes are not all is owed to me."

"Oh, I forgot about that, Mr. Mendoza. You owe the fee for getting the job."

"I missed some work a while back, because I got sick."

"Excuses, excuses, I don't want to hear it woman."

"Look, Mr. Mendoza, ever since my husband passed, I've been doing my best to take care of my daughter."

"I don't want to feel sorry for you, Bertha, because I would have to feel sorry for others."

"I'm not looking for any pity, Mr. Mendoza. I am just asking for a little more time to pay my fees."

"Well, I see something very pretty I like maybe we can come up with a deal, huh, Bertha?"

"Mr. Mendoza, get out of my home, get out!"

"Alright, alright, but let me tell you something, woman, if you don't pay me, your daughter won't have a mother."

"Don't threaten my mama, Mr. Mendoza. Get out now!"

"Alright, but remember what I said."

"You better pay up, Bertha."

"I will be back, huh, huh. Mr. Mendoza left the house with such a sense of empowerment."

"Ma that means man threatened you, I'm scared."

"Don't worry, Tara, I will get the rest of the money somehow."

"Everything will be alright. That Mr. Mendoza own everything in town and everybody."

"He is so evil, ma; I hate that man."

"Don't worry about Mr. Mendoza, Tara, he will get his someday."

Chapter 3

"Hey, Jake."

"Yes, sir, Mr. Mendoza."

"This young man here must be your son?"

"Oh, yes, sir, this is my boy, Erick."

"How old is Erick?"

"He's sixteen, sir."

"I must remember that; it is my business to know everybody and everything."

"Oh, yes sir, Mr. Mendoza, everybody in town knows who you are."

"Yeah, that's right, Erick, everyone does know."

"Now I am not to make nice, how long will you be off from work, Jake?"

"Well, Mr. Mendoza, I'm still recovering from my hip surgery."

"Well, I don't like it when someone is off work for so long."

"But Mr. Mendoza, when my hip is healed, I will come back to work."

"How much time do you need to heal, Jake?"

"A couple of months, sir! A couple of months!"

"You got to be crazy if you think I'm going to allow you that kind of time off work."

"But Mr. Mendoza, I fell off the ladder on the job."

"You better return to work in two weeks, Jake."

"Two weeks! How can I get back to work in two weeks Mr. Mendoza?"

"You find a way Jake, two weeks, that's all!" At that time, the look on Jake's face was hopelessness.

"But that's impossible. I can't return to work in two weeks."

"You do as I say or you are done, you hear me, done!"

"Oh no, Mr. Mendoza, have a heart please, sir!"

"Stop crying like a girl. Be a man!"

"Why are you making my father beg and cry, Mr. Mendoza? Everyone is afraid of you, but all I see is a fat evil pig! You are a pig and you are slime!"

"My, my, your son has a temper, Jake."

"Do you know who you are talking to, boy?"

"Yeah, an evil fat jerk. You treat people like dirt. You don't have a heart. I'm not afraid of you, pig, I'm not! My dad can barely walk, yet you are threatening him. You are an evil bully."

"Erick, Erick, be quiet! Mr. Mendoza, he didn't mean what he said."

"My boy has a little temper You know how kids are."

"Yeah, your boy has a big mouth and I'm going to have to shut him up someday."

"Oh no, it won't happen again, I promise."

"Well, it better not, Jake, remember you only have two weeks to report back to work. If not you and this big mouth son of yours will be homeless as well as the rest of your family! Have a nice day, Jake!"

Mr. Mendoza walks away, Jake's eyes focusing on him until he disappears into the evening light.

"Erick, I know you love me and want the best for me, but you can't talk to Mr. Mendoza like that. He owns this town; and is a very dangerous man. I don't want to lose you, son. Just keep quiet, promise me okay."

"I promise just for you, just for you."

"Don't be afraid of Mr. Mendoza, you know you can't go back to work in two weeks."

"I must and I will, son, I have no choice, I have no choice."

"This isn't right for one evil bully to own this town."

"Well, Erick, there are things in the world that is not fair."

"Someone needs to stop Mr. Mendoza, before he hurts someone."

"I agree son, but who, who is brave enough to do that?"

"Promise me that you will never tell your mother and sister about this Erick, promise!"

"I promise, Dad, I won't tell anyone."

"You are a good boy, Erick, I'm proud of you."

"You are a good dad, the best dad ever." Erick knew he wouldn't keep that promise to his dad he only wanted to ease his mind so he wouldn't worry.

"Don't worry, son, go and have fun with your friends. You kids like to hang out and have fun! You are kids! Go have fun!"

Chapter 4

"What's up, Erick, why the sad look on your face?"

"Jeremy, you don't want to know."

"Yes, I do, Erick, I'm your best friend and you can tell me anything."

"It's Mr. Mendoza. He is the devil!"

"You bet he is. He owns everything in town and everybody."

"He must be putting the squeeze on your dad, huh."

"Yeah, Jeremy, he is."

"The same here, he is abusing my dad too, and I had to watch it."

"How could one man own everything and everyone in this town?"

"I feel so helpless, Jeremy, like I'm useless."

"I feel helpless too. We can't do anything about it."

I feel like leaving this miserable town right now!

"If you runaway, Jeremy, it will break your parents' hearts."

"Yeah, I guess you're right, so I won't. Hey, here comes, Tommy, Tara, Emily and Jessie! Let's keep quiet about this."

"Hey guys what's happening? What's going on? Hey, Jeremy and Erick, you guys want to do something?"

"Yeah, what do you all have in mind?"

"Let's go to the arcade and play some video games." All the teens gathered their things and headed down the street to the arcade.

"Look, there's Remy Mendoza, Mr. Mendoza's son."

"Great, we can't even come to the arcade and not run into a Mendoza."

"Right, Erick, maybe we should get out of here."

"No, Tommy, we are not going to leave just because of Remy Mendoza."

"Tara is right, we are not going to be cowards. We didn't bother anybody."

"Yeah, we have a right to go wherever we want."

"Right Jeremy, we don't have to be afraid of the Mendoza's."

"Look he's coming."

"Remy, he is coming over here!"

"What do we have here! The six goofballs! Why are you here?"

At that time, the teens looked around at one another in disbelief.

"Can't you all talk? Don't worry, I'm not here to make you all sweat, but I do want a smile from you pretty girl." Tara knew that comment was directed to her, she became nervous.

"Remy, we're here to just play some video games, okay! We don't want any trouble."

"Look who's talking, Jeremy, you look nervous every time I see you BOO!"

I'm not afraid of you, Remy, I just don't want any trouble, alright?"

Out of nowhere a soft voice said, "Yeah, why don't you go back to where you came from, Remy."

"Wow! Who are you? You're really cute. Is your name Tara?"

"None of your business, I want you to get out of my face, Remy Mendoza!"

"What! You think you're too good for me or something?"

"I just don't want to look at your face Remy so just leave us alone."

"Well, let me tell you something, Tara. My father owns this whole town and also your parents. My father is THE MAN! We are rich and you all are poor, so you all are beneath us!"

"I'm better than you swines, you poor flunkies. I'm a Mendoza!" Jeremy tried to keep quiet but couldn't.

"Yeah, your father is rich, but he steals from everybody in town and he is a bully."

"And you are just like him, a bully and so full of yourself."

Oh, look at Jeremy working up the nerve to talk to me. Tara soon joined Jeremy to help defend everyone.

"Go away and leave us alone, Remy!"

"Tara, Tara, you are so feisty. I will remember this. And as for the rest of you, especially miss big mouth Tara, you're all a bunch of losers."

"Remember, my father owns all of you people including your parents and everything in this town! We can do anything to you and them!" Tara shouted.

"We don't want you here, so just go away, Remy!" Emily also expressed to him.

"Like Tara said, go away, Remy. You're not wanted here!"

Okay, so it's like that huh? I'm out of here!" Remy walks out of the arcade slowly as if his weight restricts his movement.

"Glad he's gone, and I hope we never see him again."

"Tara, it is best to just ignore him, but sometimes your temper gets the best of you."

"Emily, you are the silent one so I'm just making up for your lack of responses."

"Forget about Remy Mendoza, Tara." All the teens left the arcade feeling intimidated.

Chapter 5

"Ma, why are you so sad, what happened?"

"Don't worry about it, Jessie, everything's alright." Jessie knew her mom wasn't telling her everything.

"No, it isn't ma, now tell me what's wrong or I will worry more."

"Okay, but this is my problem, not yours Jessie."

"Mr. Mendoza wants me to go out with him on a date, if I don't, he will make me pay more on my monthly fee."

"He wants you to date him, Ma?" Jessie looked confused.

"Yes, if I don't, he will make me miserable. I don't know what else to do."

"He can't force you, Ma." Jessie can't believe what she is hearing.

"I'm afraid he can and he will, Jessie. Ever since your father left us, it's been just you and I. I work hard for the two of us." Jessie's mom had a small tear trickle down her cheek, then she turned her face so her daughter couldn't see it.

"Don't do it, Ma! Don't let him make you do anything you don't want to do."

"I have no other choice, Jessie." Jessie's mom thought to herself that the world is so unfair.

"I hate Mr. Mendoza, I hate him, I hate him!" Jessie could feel her emotions to cause her face to heat up.

"Jessie, he isn't worth hating."

"Well, I can't help it, I hate him!"

"Well, I'm going to do it, I will go on the date with him and maybe he will leave us alone, and that will take care of what I owe him."

"Isn't he married, Ma?" Again, Jessie had a confused look on her face.

"Yes, he is, but that evil man gets what he wants." The shame Jessie's mom felt as she expressed the situation to her daughter she felt trapped in.

Jessie's eyes were now filling with tears, and it was nothing she could do about the problem they had with Mr. Mendoza.

"Honey, I can see this is upsetting you, so we won't talk about it anymore, okay! I will be alright." Jessie knew it wouldn't be easy for her to forget about the pain she and her mom were in. She also thought, Maybe I should go to Mr. Mendoza house and plea to him to stop bothering my mom, to go on a date with him and maybe, just maybe he will have mercy.

Jessie leaves the house an indeed ends up at Mr. Mendoza's house.

Chapter 6

"Who are you, girl?"

"My name is Jessie, Mr. Mendoza." She really didn't want to address him with respect, but she knew she had to be as nice as she could be.

"Mr. Mendoza, it just me and my ma. My father left us, so ma works hard to take care of us, she doesn't need more stress. Can you leave her alone and not force her to go on a date with you?" Jessie was hoping she wouldn't break down and cry she wanted to show courage while she was in his presence.

"Please, Mr. Mendoza, she is a good woman." Jessie crosses her fingers hoping he will listen to her plea.

"So, you want me to let your ma, as you call her, out of an agreement?"

"Mr. Mendoza, it is not an agreement, when something is forced on someone, I wouldn't call that an agreement." Jessie sighed.

"Well, girl, I got a suggestion. How about you take her place?" Jessie gulped, not really knowing what to say.

"Take her place! Why, Mr. Mendoza? I'm only sixteen years old."

"Who's counting, girl! Remember, I'm the law in this town, do you understand?"

"Please, Mr. Mendoza, have a heart please, please, please!"

"You get out of here now and don't come back ever!"

"But you haven't heard a word of what I said."

"Yeah, I heard what you said but it doesn't matter. Now get out of here, and if you ever come back, the next time I won't be so nice."

Chapter 7

Jessie meets up with her friends. "I'm so upset. I don't know what to do."

"What's wrong, Jessie?"

"Mr. Mendoza. Is forcing my mom to go out with him or she could lose her job." Tara is thinking how one man controls everyone in town.

"That evil man, he always thinks he could have his way with anybody and everybody in this town."

"Guys, I just left Mr. Mendoza. I begged him to leave my mom alone but he just laughed at me. He told me to get out and not to come back or else. My pleading didn't mean anything to him." All the teens had sad looks on their faces.

"We knew he was evil, but he's even more evil than we thought." They all agreed.

"That man is the devil himself. We must do something to stop him."

"Jeremy, we are just teenagers. We're helpless." Tara sighed.

"I would like to rip his throat out. I want his head on a platter."

"I know you do, Tara, we all want the same thing, but we are kids and he has people to protect him."

"Tara, you do have a terrible temper, we worry about you." Emily looks at her with concern.

"Yeah, Tara, we don't want you to go and try to do something foolish." All the teens express their concerns about Tara's temper.

"Yeah, we all have to stick together. We are all friends. Emily again is trying to convince her friend to listen to them."

"Alright, guys, I promise that I won't do anything foolish, we are all victims in this city."

"Yes, we are Tara, we're all helpless victims."

"Hey, how about we all go to a movie so we can forget about our problems." Jessie hopes her friends agree to the movie.

"Hey, what's happening to Emily? She's throwing up! Her body's shaking all over!"

"It's probably her nerves. We're all very nervous."

"Yeah, Tommy, we got to get it together."

"We can't even enjoy being teenagers. We're nervous wrecks!"

"Okay, Jessie, your idea of going to the movies is a good one. Let's go!" The teens headed down the long road hoping to leave their worries behind.

"Oh no, there's Remy Mendoza's girlfriend. She's a trouble maker too."

"Hey guys, or should I say gang of six stooges or six idiots. Yeah, I'm talking to all of you!" The friends know they will all have to defend each other once again.

"Hey four eyes, isn't your name, Emily? Those glasses you're wearing makes you look smart, but you're probably dumb, huh?"

"Hey, leave her alone, we're not bothering you!"

"What's your name? Oh, I know the whore of Riverside!" Tara is now steaming.

"That's not funny." It is hard for Tara to control her temper, so she takes a deep breath and remembered what her friends said about her temper. "I heard about you, your name is Tara and you have a big mouth."

"Oh yeah? Well, I know you're Remy Mendoza's girlfriend, so why don't you pick on someone that is not afraid of you, Emily is not a fighter, but I am!"

"Get out of my face, you whore!" Mendoza's girlfriend felt a little strange that someone stood up to her and that rarely occurs.

"I'll get you, Tara, I'll see what Remy has to say about all of you!" At that time, Remy's girlfriend left, you could hear the gasp Emily made and the relief she expressed with her face.

"Tara, you can't hold your temper. We got enough problems. Why did you say that to her?"

Tara kept quiet and thought to herself, and wished her friend had courage like she did.

"I'm tired of being stomped on and the rest of you should be too!"

"But, Tara, you know we are helpless. Mr. Mendoza is powerful. He can get his goons to beat us up." Erick is now frustrated and scared.

"Yeah, Erick, we might be helpless, but we don't have to be sitting ducks."

"So, what can we do, Tara, what can we do?"

"Nothing, nothing. I'm sorry, guys, I'm so frustrated, and I don't know what I am saying."

"She called us losers. Maybe we are." Emily is holding her head down.

"Oh, come on, you guys, we might be helpless but we're not losers." Tara wants to reassure her friends and hope she will have a positive impact on them. Erick tried his best to remain silent, but he couldn't.

"I'm so afraid for my dad, I don't know what to do."

"Don't cry, Erick, don't cry," Jessie shouted!

"I'm so afraid for my mom. I can't save her."

"Jessie not you too. Erick made it known that Jessie was not alone, our lives are miserable. We can't help our parents or nobody."

"Let's face it, guys, we are helpless."

"Tommy, why say those things?" Emily had enough nerve to confront Tommy.

"I'm just saying what is true, Emily."

"Well, we are just young, but we have seen misery. Enough misery for a lifetime."

"We should leave this miserable town."

Erick also commented, "If we all leave this town now, it will certainly disappoint our parents and also break their hearts, Tommy."

"We are doomed, we just have to be miserable."

"You may be right Erick, but we are just helpless teenagers."

Chapter 8

"Come on, guys, let's just go for a walk and cool our heads." Jeremy had a smile on his face hoping his friends would feel better if they saw the positive look on his face.

"Hopefully, we can walk without running into anybody connected to Mr. Mendoza."

"Yeah, Jeremy, but we're at the end of town and it's getting dark."

"Man, you're right, Erick!"

As the teens proceeded along the foggy field, Erick said, "Hey look, there's some kind of light up ahead."

"Yeah, I see it." Emily acknowledged!

"What the heck it that?"

"I don't know." The teens were all curious.

"I can't see well at night. You guys know that without my glasses, I can't see well at all."

"It's straight ahead, Emily, do you see it now?"

"Yeah, I see something."

"I'm scared." Emily is now shaking and saying she wants to go home.

"Just calm down, Emily, there's nothing to be scared about."

"Come on, guys, let's see what it is."

"Uh, uh, I got a bad feeling about this."

"Oh, come on, Emily," Jeremy still trying to reassure everyone, "we're all going together, aren't we? We'll be fine."

"What is this? It looks like a lantern or something."

"You're right, Tara, I think it is a lantern."

"Hey, it's opening up!" The voice was loud and clear.

"What is your command?"

"It's talking to us, you guys."

"Tell me what you want and I will grant your wish." The teens were amazed by what they had found.

"Who and what are you?" Tara demanded an answer!

"I am the all-powerful lantern; your wish is my command!"

"We must be dreaming because no lantern can talk."

"I am the all-powerful lantern. I see that you all are in need of help."

"It's real, we're not dreaming." Tara now believed what was before her.

"Okay lantern, you're here to help us how?"

"Whatever is your command, I will grant."

"You're saying that you can grant all six of us any wish?"

"Yes, any wish to each and every one of you."

"Okay lantern, all of us are sad about this evil guy who controls the town. He abuses us and our parents."

"Okay, lantern, but first let us introduce ourselves."

"I'm Jeremy."

"I'm Tara."

"I'm Erick."

"I'm Jessie."

"I'm Tommy."

"Well, Emily, say something to the lantern."

"Man, I'm scared. I'm Emily."

"Now what is a wish that I can grant to you all?"

"What can we do to stop Mr. Mendoza?" Tara didn't hesitate to ask that question. Some of the teens gave Tara a puzzled look.

"Jeremy, the lantern said it will grant us any wish."

"Tara, are you sure we can ask that of him?" Tara without any hesitation said yes.

"Well books, movies and tales about powerful vampires sounds good to me," Tara says, "how about asking the lantern to turn us into vampires?"

"Vampires? Tara, really? We would have to kill people by sucking their blood!" Jeremy looked uneasy about this.

"Nope, I'm not with that either, Jeremy."

Emily also disagreed and said, "Yuck! Just the thought of something like that makes me sick."

"To be a vampire, we would have to be dead and I don't want to be dead, Tara."

"Me neither, I don't want to be no Count Dracula, no way."

"But you guys, vampires are very powerful, and they can't be stopped. If we ask the magical lantern to turn us into vampires, then we can protect our families and destroy Mr. Mendoza and his armies."

"But vampires? Blood sucking vampires?"

"No, Jeremy, we will ask the lantern to make us vampires that don't suck blood." Tara was very excited, "Do you know about vampires that don't suck blood?" Tara didn't answer, but she knew it wouldn't matter one way or another.

"Hey, think about it, you guys, vampires that are very powerful and can't be defeated by anything. They can't be stopped by crosses or silver bullets."

"I agree with Tara. We could be very powerful and save our families from Mr. Mendoza." Jeremy was excited now.

"What do you think, guys?"

"Well, Tara, if that lantern would give me perfect eyesight, I wouldn't have wear glasses anymore."

"Oh, Emily, is that all you wish for?" Emily smiled.

"How 'bout it, guys, do we ask together to the magical lantern to turn us into vampires?"

"Yes, we will all ask together." Everyone agreed.

"Magical lantern, our wish is that you turn us all into vampires who don't suck blood to survive."

"Vampires that can't be defeated by anything. That's what we all wish for."

"I will grant you all your wishes. And since this was your idea, Tara, I the magic lantern will make you the most powerful vampire of all."

"Thank you, magical lantern." At this time, a rumble of thunder that was so loud the ground beneath them shook and when the teens tried to make sense of it all their eyes started rolling back in their heads without any control.

When they all regained their composer, the loud powerful voice said, "Your wish has been granted. I shall leave you all now."

"I feel different. I feel very energetic. I feel so strong." All the teens agreed about the changes they felt.

"Look at how fast I am, Erick."

"Yeah Jeremy, look! I can fly, I can fly."

"Yeah, me too Jessie."

"Look, I pushed this tree down with one arm, Tommy."

"Look, I can pick up this truck very easily." All the teens were very excited by the powers they now had.

"This is great, ha, ha! I love it! I love being a vampire!"

"Hey, Emily, let's see what you can do."

"I can fly like the rest of you guys. Look I just punched a hole in this rock, ha ha!"

"Come on Tara, show us your powers. The magic lantern said you are going to be the most powerful vampire. So, let's see what you got."

"I can fly like all of you guys too."

"What else can you do, Tara?" Emily was eager to know.

"Look, I can pick up this tree out of the ground!"

"I can pick up this truck with one hand and throw it out of sight."

"Look, I can move faster than all five of you guys."

"Wow, Tara, we are fast but you are faster than the speed of sound. Wow!"

"Look, I can blow my breath and large objects like trees, trucks, houses will move."

"Hey, watch what I can do with that bush using my eyes."

"Oh wow, Tara, you just set that bush on fire using your eyes."

"Wow Jeremy, look at what Tara can do with her eyes. We can't do that!"

"Nope, you can't. I can also make fire come out of my mouth."

"Take a look at that rock over there. I made it burn, see!"

"I can't set anything on fire with my eyes or my mouth."

"Tara, you are truly greater than the rest of us. You're unstoppable."

"No Jeremy, we are all unstoppable. We're not just invincible. There's nothing that can defeat us. We can do anything! We are vampires!"

"That's right, Tara, we are vampires."

"Alright! We're vampires! Look at the things we can do!"

"Yep guys, we are so strong, there is nothing we can't do!"

"It's almost like a dream, guys! We're vampires!"

"And I don't have to wear my glasses anymore. This is great!"

"Yep Emily, since you're a vampire now, you don't need glasses."

"This is not real; we must be dreaming. Tara insisted that it was real."

"How do we know this is real, Emily?"

"The magic lantern granted our wishes. We wanted to be vampires and now we are."

"Look guys, this is our destiny. We found the magic lantern and won't have to worry anymore about our problems."

"Yeah Tara, you're right. All six of us have been worried about our parents. Now the teens all agreed their worries are now in the past."

"We are not human anymore. We are vampires and we're very powerful."

"Yep Jessie," Tara explained, "we fear no one. We have the power to defend ourselves."

"A miracle has happened. We are vampires, and we don't have to suck blood to survive," Tara reminded her friends.

"Yes, we know our objective and that is to destroy our enemy, Mr. Mendoza."

"Let's put our hands together and make a vow that we will destroy Mr. Mendoza."

"So why are we wearing our regular clothes?"

Tara responded, "You're right, Erick, like in the movies, the tough guys wear leather."

"Yeah, black leather! Hey, we have these powers, let's put them to use by breaking into a store and stealing some leather outfits."

"We don't have any money, so that would be a good plan."

Everyone agreed, "Let's go, guys." The teens went to town and did exactly what they said, steal.

"Wow, Tara, you look like a million bucks in that leather outfit."

"Yours fit you well also, Jessie. We're rocking in our leather."

"Let's go and see what Mr. Mendoza will think of us now."

"Yeah, let's go." The teens headed back through the foggy field past their neighborhoods to make it to Mr. Mendoza's place.

Chapter 9

Mr. Mendoza makes his way to Mrs. Olgilbee house. She is now terrified because she knows the threats that are about to come.

"Do you have my money? Remember the loan from the bank."

"Oh, Mr. Mendoza, I pay your bank every month. I don't know if you're aware of this Mrs. Olgilbee, but my rates have gone up, so you must pay me more money."

"Please, Mr. Mendoza, I'm seventy-five years old, I'm on a pension and I can't possibly pay you extra, I can only pay what the bank's agreement is."

"You pay what I say you pay, Mrs. Olgilbee! Don't you ever forget that! I don't care especially if they are either elderly or poor. I have no sympathy for you or anybody else. So that you understand, this is not personal, only business." Mrs. Olgilbee is now sobbing.

"Do you think I manage to run this town by giving people a break? Now, you have until six o'clock this evening to come up with my money or else, I'll bring my men to clear you out of here!" Mr. Mendoza leaves but before he did, he stared Mrs. Olgilbee in the eyes to put fear in her and he did.

"That evil, evil man! I can't pay him in that short of time! What will I do? What will I do? I need help, what am I gonna do?" Mrs. Olgilbee kept sobbing. Six o'clock came and Mr. Mendoza shows up and pushes open the door.

"It is six o'clock, lady, do you have my money?"

"Please have mercy, don't take my home. I don't have any more money." Mr. Mendoza reminds the old lady what would happen, she was still begging and sobbing for quite some time. Minutes went by and finally the men arrived. "Please have mercy, don't take my home." She pleaded again!

"Too bad ma'am, but we got our orders to remove you and everything out of this house."

"You can't remove me. I'm an old lady. Don't touch me! Let me go! Let me go! Help me! Help me!" The teens were almost at Mr. Mendoza's place when they could hear commotion in the distance.

"Hey, you hear that, guys? The power of hearing is the greatest. We are at least a mile away." Tara knew the sounds they were hearing meant trouble.

"It sounds like someone is asking for help."

"Somebody helps me, please!" Mrs. Olgilbee cried out. The teens are now in the old lady's front yard.

"Oh my! Where did you kids come from?"

"I'm Tara, and these are my friends. We heard your cries for help. What's wrong?"

"There are two evil men in my house, and they threw me out of my own home. They work for that evil Mr. Mendoza. I went to the bank for a loan because my roof was old and leaking water. I needed the money to repair the roof. The loan is paid every month, yet Mr. Mendoza raises the interest of the loan. I'm on a pension and it's very hard for me to pay more. But he doesn't care, and that's why he sent his men to put me out. I'm a defenseless old woman. I can't fight Mr. Mendoza. He owns everything in town. I don't know what to do.

Look, they're throwing all my belongings out of the house. Look at what they're doing!"

"Okay, just stay out here. We'll take care of this. What's your name, ma'am?"

"I'm Mrs. Olgilbee. What were your names again?"

"I'm Tara and this is Tommy, Emily, Jessie and Erick." Tara tells them she is going inside and for the rest of them to stay with Mrs. Olgilbee, Tommy didn't feel comfortable letting Tara go in alone. "Go on, Tommy, stay with Mrs. Olgilbee?"

"Hey, wait a minute. Don't you think I should go in there with you?"

"No, Tommy, stay with Mrs. Olgilbee and the others." Tara kicks the door open without any fear.

"Who are you, girl, get out of here."

"We have business to take care of now get out of here now!"

"I'm not going anywhere. I'm going to tell you two just once to leave now." Tara eyes were now glowing a bright green color.

"Leave," Tara warned them, "or else."

"Huh, huh, can you believe this kid? You've got a lot of nerve, girl!"

"Why don't you get out this is adult business. Not high school." Tara spun around with remarkable speed; things went flying everywhere.

"Ouch! Ow! Don't." Tara grabbed the man around the neck and snapped it.

"Why, you little bitch! You just killed my partner! Now I'm going to kill you! Gun shots rang throughout the house. What the hell? I just shot you ten times! Not even a scratch! Who are you?"

"I'm your worst nightmare!"

SNAP! The two men were now dead. Tara felt a sense of accomplishment.

"Alright Tommy, bring Mrs. Olgilbee in now, everything will be fine."

"Oh, my goodness! What is this? They're dead! But how did you do this?"

"I just know how to fight."

"But they had guns! I heard shots, yet you're not even bleeding! I thought it's impossible to stop them."

"Who are you two kids, and where did you come from? I don't think I got your name, young lady."

"I'm Tara."

"Mrs. Olgilbee, you're safe now."

"But these two men worked for Mr. Mendoza and he's going to be very angry when he finds out that his two men are dead. He's going to come after me now."

"Don't worry, Mr. Mendoza won't bother you again, we promise."

"How could I be assured that Mr. Mendoza will not come after me?"

"Don't worry, Mrs. Olgilbee, mark my word," Tara pleaded.

"But you are just kids! Mr. Mendoza has a lot of power and you can't stop him."

"Mrs. Olgilbee, didn't I prove to you that we are not to be messed with."

"Yes, but I'm very confused, how could a teenage girl kill two armed men?"

"I took some martial arts lessons, Mrs. Olgilbee."

"You must be really good at it because those men had guns."

"I know but I was much swifter than they were," Tara lied.

"Thank you, kids, for helping me, but I know Mr. Mendoza will come after me eventually."

"Don't worry about it, Mrs. Olgilbee, go back inside your house."

"But, what about those dead men in the house?"

"We'll take care of that, Mrs. Olgilbee." Tara goes inside the house and pick up each of the men with her left and right hand and flies away with them and drops the bodies in Riverside Lake, while the others were close behind her. When they all landed, Tommy asked when the others were not around.

"Hey, Tara, how did you kill those two men so quickly?"

"Well, Tommy, all I did was snap their necks. My speed is unreal. I'm so fast, a mere human couldn't see me. The one guy shot at me ten times, but the bullets just bounced off me. I love feeling so powerful. You know, guys, there are no limits to our powers."

"Yes, especially yours, Tara. You are the most powerful of all of us."

"Well, guys, that's because I was the chosen one who had the most courage and faith in the magic lantern."

"Come on, let's get back on the path to Mr. Mendoza's place."

"Yeah, Tara, let's. Can you believe what we've done?"

Tommy replied, "We have experienced our first adventure as vampires." The teens all agreed what they did made them feel good and powerful.

"So did we really help her by killing those two men?"

"Well of course, Emily, what a dumb question." Tara looked at Emily with amazement.

"Well, actually Tara did the dirty work. She killed both men."

Tommy said, "All we did was watch after the old lady."

The teens replied, "What did you actually do, Tara? How did you kill those men?"

"Emily, do you really want to know, you promise you won't pass out? It was easy. I snapped both their necks. One guy shot at me ten times, but the bullets just bounced off me. You see there is not even a scratch on me. Man, that was fun."

Chapter 10

"Wow, Tara, you did have fun, but the rest of us haven't been in battle yet." Meanwhile, Jeremy and Erick pick up sounds with their powerful ears from miles away that Mr. Mendoza was at the local diner stuffing his face with food at the same time criticizing everyone in the diner.

"That evil fat pig! He just keeps bulling everyone in town. He has to be stopped."

"But, Erick, we will get him very soon."

"No, Jeremy, we are not going to get Mr. Mendoza soon. We are going to have some fun with him."

"What do you mean by that, Tara?"

"We'll start by killing the rest of his men, and then we'll save him for last."

"We'll scare him! We will taunt and intimidate him. I want him to feel helplessness, I want to do to him what he has done to the people of this town."

"Yeah, Tara, that's a good idea. Let him suffer and then we'll kill him."

"No, Jeremy, we will keep him alive, we will bring justice to our town."

"We are going to tear Mr. Mendoza inside out." Tara was now more serious than ever.

Chapter 11

"Tara, you are more powerful than all of us, so I think you should be the leader," Jessie explained.

"Leader, why do we need a leader?"

"Come on, Tara, we must have a leader. Let's vote on it." Emily felt since everyone were vampires, they were equal and that no one should be in control over another.

"Look. Emily, we all are vampires and we're a team. We do need a leader." Jeremy thought it should be him since he was a boy and also the biggest.

"But, Jeremy, Tara is the most powerful and she's the smartest." Okay, finally they all agreed it would be Tara.

"Yeah, Jeremy, Tara is the most powerful and we do need a leader."

"You really think so, Erick?"

"Yep, Jeremy, now let's vote. All in favor of Tara being the leader, raise their hands."

"All approved!"

"It's unanimous. Tara has been voted leader."

"Oh, go ahead and make her the leader, but remember we are a team of vampires." Emily seemed annoyed.

"Look, Emily, you may think we're all equal, but we do need leadership." Tara went on with authority and no hesitation.

"I have fire, the brains, and the temperament to be cautious in mapping our destruction."

"We will hunt down Mr. Mendoza's men and I will personally destroy them. The likes of them will never be seen anymore."

"Mr. Mendoza will also be destroyed from the inside out."

"Wow, Tara, from the inside out, what are you going to do?" Jessie asked.

"Yeah, Tara, are you going to give Mr. Mendoza a great kill, huh?"

"Friends, Mr. Mendoza must be last. Last represents final judgment and there is no other method of fear than to know he is last to go."

"Wow, what makes you have such deep thoughts, Tara?" Jessie asks.

"It must be our vampirism. We are of great strength but our minds are stronger, friends."

"I know I feel stronger in every way. All of us are different, we all are stronger than ever before."

"Our identity remains only within ourselves know can really know our secret."

"Our mission is to only get Mr. Mendoza's men, those thugs are the first to be destroyed."

"We do not interfere with other crimes unless there is a serious danger to an innocent person." Tara made that perfectly clear. We will never allow ourselves to get too emotional. This is when we will not be at our best.

"Our imagination when being in battle for our powers are unlimited." Tara goes on.

"Our families shall never know our secret. It could be manipulated if discovered."

"When a child is in danger from a human, never kill in front of them; we don't want children to be afraid of us. That will be some of the rules of our group, this is our oath. The teens all nodded in agreement. Go and be vampires of hope that will fight for peace for all the town people."

Chapter 12

Later on that evening, one of the police officers arrived at Mr. Mendoza's house to tell him two bodies were found in Riverside Lake, and that they were employees of his.

Mr. Mendoza looked furious.

"Who did this? Who killed my men, who will kill my men? I want to know I will have somebody's head. I will turn this town of inside out. I own this town. I am the big man in this town. You hear me!"

"I am Beebee Mendoza. I can do whatever I want. How dare anyone challenge me, when they killed my men that was a threat against me. I will go house to house. Until I get an answer. I am the boss. Me! The big man! The man that owns all of the fools in this town." The police officer was now shaking, he also was on Mendoza's payroll.

"I'm sending the rest of men out to help me search this entire town until we find out who killed my men. I need to know who my enemy is. The men who were killed were to put that old woman out of the house that should be mine now." Mrs. Olgilbee was sitting by the window in her rocker when she saw two men approaching her property.

She shouted, "Why are you men here, go away!"

"Our boss sent us here because two of his men were found dead with their necks snapped. We believe you know something, so start talking old lady."

"I don't know anything. I don't know what you are talking about. Get out of my house."

"We know the men were here earlier to put you out and now they're dead!" The men were now walking around the old lady in circles.

"Go away, go away, you are bad men, leave me alone." Mrs. Olgilbee is begging and crying.

"Now we are going to make you talk old lady."

"Oh no please don't, don't hurt me!"

"Take this, old lady." One of the men slaps the old lady across her face. "It hurts don't? I will slap you again unless you talk."

"Talk, old lady, I'm just getting started."

"Yeah, we're just getting started old lady."

"Help, help, help me somebody." The old lady is begging on her knees.

"Look, this foolish old woman thinks somebody can hear her."

Chapter 13

"Tara, what's wrong?"

"Jessica, I hear someone crying out, I need to go we can finish our talk later. Do you want us to come, no!" The teens ask.

"I will go alone." Tara's extraordinary hearing power can make her hear many miles away. Suddenly, Tara appears at Mrs. Olgilbee's house.

"Who are you, girl? Where did you come from?" Tara's eyes became bright green, while her eyes rolling in the back of her head, a sudden power came upon her furniture moving around everywhere; the men were being tossed around like rag dolls.

"Ow, ow, where did you get your strength from?" one of the men cried out!

"Ow, ow don't, don't please, please!" The other man took out his gun and shot Tara. But nothing happened, the bullets just bounced off Tara as if she was a rubber ball.

"I just shot you why don't you die?" Still Tara never utters a word; she reaches in both men chest and rips out their hearts simultaneously.

"It's all over, Mrs. Olgilbee, you are fine now those evil men won't bother you again." Mrs. Olgilbee is trembling and weeping.

"They are dead, you killed them. Who are you, girl?"

"I will tell you again I'm Tara."

"You are not human; no normal girl can do what you did." Mrs. Olgilbee goes on and on. "Both times you were shot the bullets just bounced off you. It seems like every time I cry out, and in trouble you show up as if you can hear my cries. What are you dear girl, I won't tell anybody."

"I just have superpowers, Mrs. Olgilbee. I am a new breed vampire. I am telling you this because I know I can trust to my powers allow me to hear for miles and miles away," Tara explains. "I can hear the helpless from anywhere." Tara tells the old lady like before; she would never have to worry about her safety.

Mrs. Olgilbee says, "I was one of those helpless people, and thank you, child, for helping me."

"It's a new day, Mrs. Olgilbee, I was given these powers to make a difference. It was your feeling of helplessness that made me hear you from so far away. My friends and I will destroy all the bad men in this town." Tara felt a sense of authority.

"They are going to come back, Mrs. Olgilbee, you must leave your home. Now that two more of Mr. Mendoza's men are dead, they might become suspicious of you."

"Leave my home? I can't leave my home, I just can't, why can't you watch over me, dear child?"

"But Mrs. Olgilbee, I can't just stay guard to you, I have other battles to fight." Tara's concerned look on her face was priceless.

"I promise if you give us some time, we will make you safe permanently."

"But my home is all I've got; I can't stay away too long. Get me back as soon as you can." Mrs. Olgilbee finally agrees to leave, she contacts her sister in Georgia to tell her she's coming to stay for a while.

When Tara meets back up with her friends, Erick asks where she has been; she responded and said she eliminated one of Mendoza's men. We have been roaming the streets, hoping that we wouldn't run into anyone needing our help, and looking for you. Erick seemed troubled by what she said but remained silent. Tara asked, "Where are Jessie and Jeremy?" The teens didn't reply.

"I want to keep our identity a secret from now on we can't let everyone know what we really are," Tara explains, "it wouldn't be safe for us."

"We must go and get Jeremy and Jessie, they can't allow themselves to just wonder off whenever they felt like it."

"Jeremy, Jessie, what are you two doing?"

"Look Tara, there's two of Mr. Mendoza's men inside of that bar."

"So what are we waiting for!"

"Guys, we have to be very careful. We mustn't allow innocent people to see us get these men."

"My palms are sweating."

Jessie says, "To get those two men, we have to act now."

Wait, strike when no one is around, we can't make any mistakes of being seen." Tara saw many people in the bar other than the men.

"We understand, Tara, and the rest of us as well, Jessie and I are not stupid we can see other people in the bar," Jeremy explained very frustrated.

"Soon Mr. Mendoza won't know what hit him, so just keep patient all of you." Tara was now showing more authority. An hour passes by and all the people have left the bar, the only people left were Mendoza's men. "Tara, this would be a perfect opportunity to destroy those two men, please can we destroy them now?" Tara then agreed and said yes.

Mr. Mendoza's men are coming out alone, obviously drunk and staggering. Jessie looks at Jeremy and says, "There isn't any eyewitnesses around. We can get them now!"

"Let's get them now."

"Who are you two kids, huh, huh?"

"Go home and play games or something. Get out of our way."

"Go and do what teenagers do," one of the men responded with anger.

"We are not going anywhere. I'm Jeremy and this is Jessie, and we came to kill both of you."

"Ha, Ha, Ha! You kids are funny. You have on leather suits and look stupid stop joking around."

"Now for the last time, go away, you kids!" Both teens felt an unusual feeling come over them. Their eyes were now glowing in a bright green light, the men were being tossed around like weightless pillows, blood splattering all over the place. The boys moved so fast the men didn't have a chance. One of the men was able to get a round off from his gun, but it didn't put one scratch on the teens.

"Ow! Ow! Oh no! Aahh! POW! POW! Aaah, aaah!"

"It's over, Jessie; I just pulled his heart out of his chest."

"And Jeremy, look what I did to my victim. I took his head off. He's headless."

"Good, Jessie. These are two of Mr. Mendoza's men that are not going to continue doing his dirty work for him."

"Jeremy, we killed these two real fast. You heard how they screamed. Jeremy, he shot me four times, but the bullets just bounced off."

I repeat, "Jeremy, he shot me point blank four times and I felt nothing."

"Being a vampire is great. I love it. I love it. When the teens returned to the rest of the group, they told them how they felt when they killed Mr. Mendoza's men."

"Yeah, Jessie, this is cool being a vampire."

"I was shot four times. The bullets bounced right off me and then I pulled their hearts out. They went on and on telling the rest of the group about the ordeal."

"Bullets will bounce off all of us. We have great powers that mere mortals can't imagine," Tara explains.

"Tonight, all six of us are going to go stalking together. I found out that on Saturday nights some of Mr. Mendoza's men will be at the gambling house."

"Oh yeah, Tara, Mr. Mendoza I heard has over a hundred men that work for him," Emily shouted! "I wonder how many of his men are at the gambling place now."

"Guys, we now need to create fear in him. We need to make him uncomfortable. Mr. Mendoza has to worry now more than he's ever had too before."

"I want Mr. Mendoza to suffer. I want him to have sleepless nights. Guys, I want Mr. Mendoza to wet his pants."

"After all of this, Mr. Mendoza will die. He will never bother anyone in Riverside again."

"I get what Tara is saying. Tara, this is why you are the leader because you are the smartest." Emily smiles with pride.

"Oh, Emily, you are just saying that because Tara is a girl."

"No, Tommy. It's true, she is the smartest she always knows the right things to say, and besides that we girls have to stick together, also girls make the best leaders." Emily grins and holds her head down.

"No, guys, I am the leader because I had faith in the magic lantern and the magic lantern had given me the most power of any vampire that ever was. My powers are endless. There is nothing I can't do with my powers. I have strength of a thousand men. I can do karate and judo. I can spit fire out of my eyes and mouth. Now, you all are very powerful vampires as well, but I'm far greater. So, you must trust and believe in me and my decisions. Our mission is not to be vigilantes, but to help the helpless like we are doing We must be smart." The teens all nod with agreement.

"We can't just go out and tear the town apart to get Mr. Mendoza. We will get him, eventually," Tara goes on.

"We must not be known by our friends and families what we are doing."

Meanwhile, Mr. Mendoza and some of his men had a meeting at the gambling hall.

"Who are killing my men? I got two more men dead! Who are killing my men?" He goes on to say somebody's got to be a fool to challenge me. "I'm the boss! I'm the boss in this town! How dare anyone in this lousy town, kill my men? I want to find out who is doing this. Is there some other player in town I don't know about?" he demanded an answer.

"No, boss, there isn't another player in town. We have checked everything."

"Boss, our men are getting their heads torn off. They are getting their hearts pulled out of their chests."

"It doesn't seem human, boss."

"Boss, a lot of the guys are getting scared."

"Scared? Nobody who works for me can be scared! You tell the men that they are to hunt down who is doing this."

"But boss, we don't know who is killing them. It seems like our men are being murdered at the blink of an eye."

"I'm going to have you men go house to house and make people talk."

"Somebody's got to know something. You will make them talk. Mr. Mendoza is now shouting."

"If there is any killing done in this town, it will be done by us. How dare they kill my men in Riverside! I own this town. I own this town! I'm the boss! I'm going to kill whoever this is, now go and get me some answers." The men leave the gambling hall to find answers to the murders of their men. Mr. Mendoza is talking to himself.

"Whoever is killing my men will be put on fire, tied to a tree with their tongues cut out." Mr. Mendoza still shouting.

"I'm Beebee Mendoza! I'm the boss! I'm more powerful than anyone, I'm the one who these people in Riverside should fear! If I have to do it myself. I will start tomorrow by combing every inch of this town to find out who is killing my men. No one will escape from me. No one will challenge me. I will light fire to this town. I will get people talking." The next day, Mr. Mendoza walked the streets of Riverside and said to everyone in Riverside, there has been killing of some of my men. Somebody knows something, so somebody better talk. Mr. Mendoza growls at the people with hate. Shortly after that, more of Mendoza's men appear.

"We're the men who work for Mr. Mendoza we are going house to house until we get some answers. You people of Riverside better talk. You better tell us who is killing Mr. Mendoza's men. If nobody talks, there will be consequences to follow and I'm sure none of you will want that," one of the bad men said.

"Is anybody going to talk? You better talk! You are all fools," Mr. Mendoza shouts! Then he spots a familiar face.

"You! I recognize you! You got that teenage son named Jeremy. Don't you know anything?" he demands, you look nervous.

"Why you look so nervous? You must know something huh?"

"No, sir, Jeremy's dad cries out, I don't know anything. I am out here to see what all the commotion is about." At that time, the men set a tree on fire, hoping to put fear in the town people, and they did just that.

"Is this your son?" Mendoza asks.

"Yes, this is my son Jeremy, but he knows nothing, sir."

"Please, please, please, sir, we don't bother anyone, we do nothing wrong. We know nothing. We are just good people in Riverside, sir." Jeremy's dad is now trembling and terrified.

"What you got to say, kid? Is what your old man saying is true?"

"Yes, my father is correct. We know nothing."

"If I find out you and your dad is lying, I will come back and destroy both of you. And don't you forget it. I am Mr. Mendoza's number one man, listen carefully they call me the devil and I live by my name."

Jeremy's dad went on to explain to his son, "I know I look weak, Jeremy, and you look at me as a coward. But, I'm just a simple man who loves his family and can't fight a powerful man like Mr. Mendoza. I just don't want any trouble. I am scared of Mr. Mendoza because I don't want him to hurt you or our family. I'm sorry, Jeremy."

"Don't be sorry, Dad, I am proud of you. You are a good father. Don't ever say I look at you as a coward, because I don't." Jeremy had one tear stream down his cheek.

"Mr. Mendoza is evil, a bully and someday he will be stopped."

"Yeah Jeremy, someone is already killing his men. Maybe he will be next." Jeremy didn't say a word about what he knew he just agreed with his dad.

"It looks like Mr. Mendoza got someone out to stop him. I wonder who that person is?"

"Well, Dad, maybe the person who is after Mr. Mendoza already knows how you feel."

"What do you mean by that, Jeremy?" Jeremy never answered.

Chapter 14

Later on, that day, Jeremy ran into Tara.

"Tara, my dad and I were walking on the street because we heard a lot of commotion, then we saw Mr. Mendoza's men set a tree on fire. They shouted this is what will happen to all you if we don't get answers." Jeremy could barely speak, he seemed to be out of breath.

"They said they are going house to house to make us tell them what we knew about the murders."

"What are we going to do, Tara? You are our leader. We will just keep quiet about the murders."

"Jeremy, calm down." Jeremy was panicking by now.

He went on to say, "We are killing Mr. Mendoza's men one by one. I'm afraid they will find out about us. Tell us Tara, how will we continue this?"

"Yeah, tell us, Tara."

Tara was becoming irritated, then shouted, "Everyone, be quiet! We won't let Mr. Mendoza's men bully and harm our families or the town's people any longer, especially the leader that's called devil."

"Mr. Mendoza is very angry. He won't stop searching for the killers of his men."

Tara went on to say, "We are not going to stop either until all the bad men are destroyed."

Emily looked nervous and then said, "Tara how, how can we kill all the men?"

"Emily, you stick with me, you are so scary. My strength will rub off to you, trust me." Tara went on to finish telling her friends the plan.

"Tonight, we go out in two groups of threes. Tommy, Erick and Jessie will be one group then Me, Jeremy and Emily will be the other. Mr. Mendoza's men will be walking the streets trying to find out who's killing all of them. If we run into them. We are going to attack. We are going to give them a bloody night to remember. Mr. Mendoza is going to start sweating even more." The teens separated in two different directions, everyone was wearing black leather and blended well with the sunset.

Chapter 15

Tara's group spots some of the men.

"Look, Tara, two of Mr. Mendoza's men are bullying those people. They are pushing and shouting at them. You could hear the women cry out saying we don't know anything please! Leave us alone!"

Jeremy says, "Tara, I recognize that man. He is the guy next in line to that Devil guy. They call him Mad Dog."

"Oh really, Jeremy, he might be a 'Mad Dog', but he is going to be a dead dog."

"Jeremy, I can take them easily, but I will let you and Emily take care of them."

"Who the hell are you two teenagers? Do you know who we are? Now get out our way."

"We aren't going anywhere!"

"What did you say, boy?" You want me to cut your tongue out?"

"Now get the hell out of our way, you and this nerdy looking girl."

Before the men could say anything else, Emily and Jeremy eyes turned a bright green, their speed became remarkable. The men started swinging at them but couldn't connect. "Who are you kids why are you doing this the men were clearly afraid. Emily pounced on top of the man then you could hear a snap, he was dead.

The other man was pleading for his life. "Please don't." But Jeremy didn't listen all you could hear was sounds of pain.

"Ow! Aaah! Help! Aaaah! Aaah! No don't! Aaaah!"

Jeremy said, "We did it. They are really dead. I was quicker than you, Emily."

"No, Jeremy, I broke his neck, did you see how fast I did that?" The teens were very proud of what they done.

"I took four bullets that did nothing to me and then I tore his tongue out of his mouth," Jeremy went on very excited.

"Jeremy, Emily, you took care of them like you were supposed to do."

The teens left the scene and decided to look for others.

Chapter 16

"Let's fly around and try to find a bigger amount of Mr. Mendoza's men because I want a piece of the action next time," Tara said with enthusiasm.

"There again is that club where Mr. Mendoza's men hang out?" The teens go in for a landing without anyone noticing them, it looks like thirty men are inside. "Let's go, Jeremy and Emily. Let's get them now and have no mercy."

"Hey who are you kids, what are you doing?" Tara grabs one of the men around the neck and snaps it in a split second. Her eyes are now glowing a bright green.

One of the men was saying, "Stop, I can't see, you are blinding me with those eyes, stop!" When Jeremy wasn't looking, the man shot him. Boom! Boom! Boom! Bullets just bounced off the boy. "Why don't you die?"

"Help, help, help!" the men cried out, chairs flying everywhere, people screaming and glass breaking. Everyone is now dead.

"Boy, that was quick. All of the men are dead."

The teens all agreed.

"Emily, I killed three all by myself," Jeremy shouted. "And Tara, your speed is unreal. They're no match to you and your power."

:My speed and power is your speed and power. Let's continue to track more of his men.:

There is another one of Mendoza's men. His is by himself harassing people.

"It's your turn, Emily. He is leaving the Gilmore house. Get him now, Emily!" Tara demanded. Emily's eyes started glowing green then she began to twirl in circles dust blowing around everywhere, she pounced on top of the man. In a split second, you could hear bones cracking, she then grabbed the man around his throat he was able to get a few words out.

"Aaah! Aaaah! Aaaah! Help me! Help!"

He is dead, blood all over the place. "I just tore his throat out."

"Good job, Emily. He didn't know what hit him."

After Emily finished destroying the bad man, everyone was so proud of her, she was gaining more and more confidence.

Tara looked over and shoulder and noticed Mendoza's men pushing an old man against a tree.

"Erick, look at those men. They got that poor man up against the tree trying to get him to talk."

"Yeah Tara, that poor man is old and they are bullying him."

"You hear him? Pleading for his life. How cruel, how cruel can anyone be to do that to a human being. We have to save him."

"Yeah, you are right, Erick, you Jessie and I must go and end this quick."

"Let's go and get these bad men now." The teens' eyes began to glow again bright green, the men were blinded by the light, they were saying who's there I can't see. Before they had a chance to run the teens warped speed overpowered them and their heads were decapitated.

"Well, that's over. We killed them in seconds. Two more of Mendoza's men gone."

"Dear old man, we have just saved your life. We need you to forget our faces."

"Can you do that, sir?" the man answered,

"I will never tell anyone. I don't know who you kids are. Thank you for saving my life." The old man grabs his cane and walks away slowly into the mist of the night.

Chapter 17

"Jeremy and Emily, we are going to the deli where a lot of Mr. Mendoza's men hang out. Erick and Jessie said they were familiar with it, but we are not."

"I know where it is, don't worry, Jeremy and Emily, everyone will follow me," Tara explains, "I have powers to see things I never saw before. My sixth sense is at the highest level. We will go to that place now. We are going to strike a devastating blow to Mr. Mendoza's men tonight." The teens all assemble like a flock of birds and took off into the night skies, a few minutes went by then they appeared at the deli.

"There are his men. I will go in first," Tara says.

"How about all the Stalkers go in together, Tara?"

"Yes, we could, but my speed is faster than yours I will go in first. Give me three minutes and then Jeremy, you and Emily follow afterwards."

"Tara, it looks like over twenty of Mr. Mendoza's men are in there."

"I know, Emily, this is what makes this so much fun."

"Wait Stalkers, give me three minutes before you two come in."

"There she goes, Jeremy. Yeah, faster than the speed of light."

Tara appears in the Deli like a speed of light, she flies above the men striking them one by one, the men are now afraid and yelling.

"Who, what, what the hell, help! Aaaah! Boom, boom, boom, boom! Help!"

"Who are you? Aaaah! Aaaah!"

Boom, boom, boom, boom, boom!

Snap, snap, crack, uh! The Stalkers are wondering what is going on in the deli.

The three minutes are up; the Stalkers agreed to go in, with amazement they say to Tara, "Everyone in here is dead. You said you were going to allow us to have some action."

"Yeah, remember Tara? Give you three minutes."

"Well, we gave you three minutes and you didn't leave us one bad man."

"Yeah, Tara, you killed many men so quickly."

"Yeah, Tara, your speed is unbelievable we have never seen you that fast before."

"Sorry, Stalkers, my adrenaline was flowing."

Blood everywhere. Heads torn off, necks broken and arms ripped off their bodies. Erick couldn't believe his eyes.

"Where are the workers of this deli?" Emily seemed worried and said, "Maybe they got extremely scared and ran off. We've got to make sure our identity stays a secret."

"We don't want our parents or anyone else to know our identity." Tara went on, "If we are identified, I have the power to zap them."

"Zap them, Tara? Really, we don't have that power."

"The magic lantern gave you more power than the rest of us."

"Much more." Jessie seemed envious.

"I have more powers as I told you before because I believed in the magic lantern in the beginning, but you all had doubts."

"Come on, Stalkers, we must get out of here before someone discovers these dead me. Let's call it a night."

Chapter 18

The Stalkers get in position and flies away into the night causing a whirlwind of dust behind them. They finally arrive at the old Riverside Lake House.

"Mr. Mendoza is going to be very angry at what happened to his so-called tough men."

"Well, we won't worry about it, Emily, and did you see Tara killed so many by herself."

"Yeah, Jeremy, Tara didn't leave a whole lot for us."

"Tara's powers are super, guys," Emily said. "Jeremy's super powerful as well, but Tara's powers are much more amazing than ours."

"Hey, all of our powers are good."

"Yeah, that's true, but we are nothing like Tara."

"This is why she is the leader." All the Stalkers agreed.

Tara was sitting alone recalling everything that occurred, Erick heard something she said but couldn't quite make it out.

"What did you say, Tara?"

"I hate that Mr. Mendoza I can't wait to kill him. I want his head on a platter." The Stalkers were saying we all want a piece of Mr. Mendoza.

"We all are going to have to take names as to who will have the honor of killing him."

"Don't forget about his top henchman, Devil. I got to kill him slow and real good you guys," Tara reminded the Stalkers about this shrewd and evil man.

"Devil will be next. Since I am the leader, I want to kill him personally."

"But Tara, we should do it together."

"No, I want to kill him alone because I am the leader and that honour should be bestowed upon me," Tara explained. The Stalkers still talking about what they will do next with excitement. "You know the office building where Mr. Mendoza works, we must watch it tomorrow night and make another vicious attack." Tara went on to say.

"As your leader, I want Mr. Mendoza's top guy Devil. I want him to beg before he dies."

"Aw man, Tara, you want all the fun. Let us have more killings."

"You all will have more to come, Riverside is a bloody town now with Mr. Mendoza's men and soon him too." Tara says, "So, guys, you will all have plenty of other chances."

Chapter 19

"Last night, I had over forty of my men killed. Forty of my men killed! Who is doing this? I want somebody's head! I want some heads! This can't be just one person killing all of my men." Mr. Mendoza is now furious.

"No boss, it definitely can't be one person who's killing all of the men."

"Hell, no Devil, but if it's the last thing I do, I will find out who is doing this and I will kill like I never killed before!"

Mr. Mendoza started pacing around the room, knocking over chairs and everything in sight. He's screaming and cursing. The men are trying to calm him down but they couldn't get a word in edgewise. Then he goes on to say, "If anyone gets in my way, they will die, you hear me, die! How dare you come to my town and kill my men." He is still throwing things in site, the men are ducking to keep from getting hit from the debris, no matter what the men would do to calm him down was useless. "This has gone too far I will not be made a fool of you hear me! Never!"

Mr. Mendoza's top man, Devil, is becoming worried that he will take his anger out on him, so he stopped trying to reason with him. Mr. Mendoza started pounding himself in the chest saying, "No one has ever challenged me before

I am to be feared, Godzilla don't want to screw with me. So fine my enemies bring them to me dead or alive!" He is so furious he continues to say, "I'm going punish those cowards. You can't hide forever!" He yells, "I will find who you are and I will cut your tongue out. I will cut your eyes out. I'm going kill you, enemy. I will kill all of Riverside." He then screams at his top man, "Go and do what you do. Go and beat somebody until they talk. I'm convinced someone knows something." Devil leaves under Mendoza's command, a few minutes later he arrives at the deli. He noticed two workers he seen before at the deli were gone. I must find them now.

Devil spots a worker and calls out to him, "Hey, hey you, Salvatore Ruiz, are you the server and cook at the deli? Did you see something? You better start talking now or I am going to skin you alive. Now talk! The poor man was trembling as he spoke."

"I saw this girl. She came busting in and started attacking all the men really fast, Mr. Devil."

"You're telling me a girl, one girl, came into the deli and killed the boss men?"

"Yes, sir that is what happened. She also was flying."

"Flying? Huh, little guy, what do you think I am? Stupid? A flying girl. A flying girl you sound ridiculous."

"Yes, sir it happened so fast she flew in the deli and attacked the men very quickly. It scared me, so I got out of there. I'm still shaking thinking about it. I never in my life have seen anything like it, Mr. Devil."

Devil thought the man was lying so he started hitting him and saying, "I will teach you a lesson, I will teach you to never lie about the things that you have said."

"Ow, ow, don't hit me anymore Mr. Devil. I am telling you the truth. Don't hit me please, please. Ow, ow! No more, no more! Have mercy, Mr. Devil!"

"You think you're going to make me believe that a girl flew in our deli and killed a lot of our men?"

"You think I'm a fool? For the last time," he yells, "tell me the truth!"

"I can't tell you anymore, Mr. Devil, because I've told you the truth."

"I'm tired of beating you, stupid fool." Devil noticed his knuckles were now swollen and quite painful, he said, "You must be telling the truth."

"Yes sir, a flying girl so fast with unbelievable powers. Have mercy, Mr. Devil. No more, please sir, please!"

"Get out of my face! But remember if you are lying, I will find you. And kill you." Devil turned the poor worker a loose and thought to himself, *Could this be true, was that fool telling me the truth?* While walking away from the deli, Devil couldn't get the thought out of his head.

Could this be possible? Nah, impossible! No way! My name is Devil, and they don't call me that name for nothing. Let me go back to the deli and see if there are any clues.

He returned, started looking around and noticed the place was a mess. The seats were torn out from the floor, he thought to himself this doesn't look like the destruction of a normal man; this place is torn up. Seats are ripped out of the floor.

"Those men must have been very strong. The evidence proves that."

Devil calls his partners to help him search for more clues. The men arrived and one of the men said, "Hey, this place looks like a riot been here, I can't identify anything here everything is destroyed and unrecognizable. What are we looking for?" he asked.

Devil yelled, "Anything! Anything! We need answers." He continued to say, "The cook said a flying girl came and destroyed the men."

"I don't believe it. He's lying," the man said, "I should kill him." Devil instructed the man to leave him alone.

"Listen up, everyone, we have a new enemy in town. Someone in this town is responsible for this, we will find out who wants a piece of the action. They will be destroyed! You hear destroyed!" He continues, "Mr. Mendoza runs Riverside and I'm his number one man. I'm about to go house to house to find out who our new enemy is."

The men finally leave the deli following behind Devil as if they were his children.

Chapter 20

In the meanwhile, the Stalkers were still at the Riverside Lake House boasting about what they had done at the deli.

"My, my, we had a good night, Tara. We struck hard and fierce at the deli, what's next?" Emily asked.

"We are going to go after Mr. Mendoza's number one flunky, Devil. He is going around town harassing people. My powers are letting me see this," Tara says, "if he wants to know who is killing Mendoza's men, he will soon find out." Tara eyes began to glow, then she realized she had to control her emotions and her eyes went back to their usual color.

"Oh Tara, are we going after the heart of Mr. Mendoza, huh?" Emily asks.

"Yes," she continues, "listen, friends, we are going to put the squeeze on Mr. Mendoza and his men."

"Who should have first crack at Devil, Tara?"

"All of us are going to visit him, Jeremy. We are going to scare him because he thinks he is so tough and bad."

"I want to see the fear in his eyes before he dies."

"Yeah Tara, I want to see him beg. Beg like he never has before."

"Jeremy, I want you to snatch his tongue out of his mouth and then tear his heart out." Tara and the Stalkers huddle in a circle and began to agree to the plans she described, suddenly the teens could feel something come over them, eyes rolling back in their heads and temples pounding, everyone was wondering what was happening to them. Tara had allowed her special powers to give them fangs. She felt they now had proven their loyalty and willingness to her. "Tara! Tara!" The Stalkers yelled, "What was that?"

"Listen, everyone. Now I have given you a gift, you are now true vampires, now let's get back to business."

"Good idea, Tara."

"Now, Jeremy, Devil never used his heart anyway, so like I said I want you to rip it from his chest. His nickname fits him perfectly." Tara tells the Stalkers, "We all are going to poke fun at him before Jeremy destroys him."

"You are a good leader for us." Erick says, "I would like to bite Devil with my fangs. What's the use in being a vampire if we don't bite anyone, Tara?"

"Erick, if you or anyone wishes to bite Mr. Mendoza's men, do as you wish. It doesn't matter how we kill these evil men."

"Boy, Tara, I can't wait until we strike. I am going to tear their heads off. That is going to feel so good, guys." The Stalkers all described what they wanted to do to the men.

Erick said, "After watching Mendoza bully my parents, I want to snatch his eyes out."

"I will be next in line," says Jessie, "then I will throw him from a window."

Tara butted in and said, "Erick, you have to wait in line behind me." The Stalkers all laughed.

"Guys, we are going to get there with Mr. Mendoza, and the rest but first we have business with Devil."

"Come on, let's go and get him. I know where he is. I can smell him now."

"Wow, Tara, I hate it that your powers are greater than ours."

"Well, you shouldn't, Emily, I am the bravest of the group, so stop saying that."

Emily drops her head in shame, knowing she didn't mean to upset her friend.

"Where is he Tara? Where can we find him?" Tommy asks.

"I see visions of Devil going to Tommy's house and he is smacking Tommy's father around."

"What? He is smacking my dad around? We got to do something now, Tara! I'm going to kill him! Now he is dead! Devil is so dead!"

"No Tommy, you can't go to your house now. Your dad will see you."

"Your fangs are exposed and your eyes are glowing. No one can know we are vampires."

"I don't care, Tara. I'm tired of Mr. Mendoza and his men bullying our parents. This has got to stop!"

"Yeah, Tara, Tommy is right. We are tired of Mr. Mendoza and his henchman Devil doing his dirty work."

"Look, guys, most of Mr. Mendoza's men are dead. Our secret of being unidentified is important. Our secrecy is vital to our mission. We can't allow anyone to know we are vampires. Tommy, do you understand? Answer me I insist Devil will be dead very soon. I am the leader because the magic lantern rewarded me the most powers due to the fact I had faith in the beginning."

"Yes, Tara, I understand."

"This is bigger than any of us. We are going against evil. We can't just allow the whole town or our parents to know who we really are. Now let's go and kill Devil. We must keep our heads together. Soon all of this will be over. Mr. Mendoza's hours of being alive are getting short. We are going to continue having our mark on Mr. Mendoza as of now. So, everyone calm down. Let's go and get Devil. He is about to leave your home, Tommy."

"Gee, Tara, I'm glad that you have x-ray vision. You can see miles away. You can see all over town without being there."

"Yeah, Emily's right. I wish we had x-ray vision. We have great powers, but nothing like yours Tara." The Stalkers take off leaving a dark cloud of smoke behind. They began circling the town until they spotted their victim.

"There there's Devil. He is getting in his car. Let's follow him." The Stalkers followed devil to every home he visited.

"Tommy, it seems like your home was the last one he visited today."

"I want to go inside of my house and see if my dad's alright."

"Tommy, you can't do that I can see that your dad is fine. Let's keep following Devil."

"There he goes. He's gone inside that store. Let's wait for him to come out." The stalkers began hovering above waiting for Devil to come out of the store.

"Okay, he's coming out," one of the stalkers shouts, they noticed a beer in his hand and then he started urinating in the street.

"Man, he's foul," Jessie says. The Stalkers are all disgusted by what they have seen.

"Listen to him. He is burping; what a pig."

"Yeah, Jessie, what a pig."

Tara says, "Okay, guys, we are going to snatch him now. Let's get him."

The Riverside Stalkers zoomed down from the sky with lightning speed.

"Who the hell are you kids? Why are you dressed in all that leather?"

"Don't worry about who we are, just know you are going to die."

"Do you kids know who I am? Are you young punks threatening me, Devil? I will blow your heads off." Devil started shooting the kids one by one, nothing happened the bullets bounced off each and of them. Devil kept shooting.

"Here, take that, you punks. Die. Die punks die, why don't you die? I shot both of you ten times. Why don't you die? What the hell is going on?" Tara tells her friends to stand back, she circled the man so fast it made him dizzy. "What, wait, what are you doing?"

The man was stunned and shocked. "I am Tara, the leader of the Riverside Stalkers. Devil, I just put a web on you where you can't move."

"You! You are the ones that have been killing our men."

"Yes, we are. Let me introduce you to the rest of my group or your worst nightmare. Jeremy, Erick, Tommy, Jessie, and Emily."

"You work for Mr. Mendoza. Is that right? You and Mr. Mendoza have beaten up our families and bullying everyone in town."

"Don't you feel ashamed, Devil?"

"Ashamed! Hell no! If I get loose, I'm going cut your throats, you punks!"

"Don't you get it, Devil? You can't hurt us, we are vampires. We are a new breed of vampires that don't need blood to survive. Emily is going to take her sharp fingernails and cut your toes off. Do it now, Emily. Get him a little taste of torture."

"Aah! Aah! Aah! That hurts, you little cow! You cut four of my toes off! I'm bleeding! I'm going to kill all of you pricks! Anybody can die and you will when I get loose."

"Still talking, Devil? Alright, Jessie is going to shut you up permanently. Do it now Jessie. Open his mouth. Cut out his tongue." Jessie followed Tara order. Emily stood up and almost fainted, Erick caught her before she hit the ground.

"Ooh, ooh, ooh, he is bleeding very bad, Tara."

"Yes, he is Emily. Now, Jeremy, break his neck now."

"But, Tara, isn't that enough? He is already dead."

"No, I want his body to be tortured, Jeremy do it," Tara shouted! You could hear bone shattering on the man's body.

"Now we have just sent him to hell."

"That felt so good to break his neck. Devil won't bother anyone of our people in town anymore."

Chapter 21

"Jeremy, I wish I could have broken Devil's neck instead of you."

"Why, Emily?"

"I want to learn how to gain more confidence, feel strong and powerful and not helpless anymore." Jeremy convinced his friend that it will happen soon.

"Mr. Mendoza is really going to be angry. His number one bad guy, his flunky, is dead."

"Yes, that's what I'm counting on. To make him as angry we can. I know he will make mistakes and when he does, we will be ready for him."

Tara went on to say, "Mr. Mendoza is going to go hard after the town's people and we are going to finish his men off. I want Mr. Mendoza to really feel desperate. I want him to sweat. We are the Riverside Stalkers. We are powerful. We are great. We are the protectors of good and peace. Never will we be the symbol for helplessness. Never will we see injustice reign again. The Riverside Stalkers will revenge evil and cruelty. Helplessness will not enter in Riverside again. For the weak and helpless will be able to feel and be the strength the town's people never knew they had." Tara's eyes were glowing brighter than ever before.

"Our fathers shall never have their dignity and pride shaken by men of evil deeds. We, the Riverside Stalkers, were born out of this injustice to make life worth living."

"But Tara, Jeremy has just broken Devil's neck. Don't you think we've become the bad guys?"

"Emily, when will you learn? It is our duty to kill, stop worrying and leave it up to me to guide you." Tara is so irritated by Emily's comment she just walks away from her.

She returns and say, "No, we will never become the bad guys. We want freedom and dignity for our parents in Riverside."

"Emily, how can we free our parents? What else do you think we can we do?" Emily looks away as if she didn't want to hear what Tara was saying.

"We all watched our parents being humiliated, pushed around, and lose their pride from this very evil man. Something or somebody heard our pleas. The magic lantern answered our cries for help and gave us what we wanted. We got magic that came into our lives, so we are not the bad guys, Emily. Do you want to give up being a vampire, Emily?"

"Well, Tara, you're right, no I don't want to give up being a vampire. For the first time, I feel powerful and confident. I feel like I can do anything. I feel unbelievable, untouchable. Nothing can stop me and all of us. I'm not Emily the nerd or Emily the coward. I'm glad that we are vampires."

"Good, no time for weak knees. We have a job to finish and we will. I am going to kill Mr. Mendoza. I want him for myself."

"But Tara, all of us want to kill Mr. Mendoza," the Stalkers replied.

"This is the main reason why we became vampires."

"Tara, I want to kill Mendoza so bad I can hardly sit still."

"Me too."

"Well, Stalkers, I can see we all have something in common, when the right time comes, I will strike not a minute before." Tara went on to ask her friends if they understood and not to do anything stupid.

"Guys, guys, I am the leader so it is up to me to decide and I have. I must kill Mr. Mendoza."

"You are right, Tara. You are the leader and you are the strongest and most powerful. We obey you, Tara."

"Okay then that's what I like to hear. Mr. Mendoza will find out soon that Devil is dead. He will feel the heat. He will get desperate and more evil."

"Are we going to kill more of his men tonight, Tara?"

"Yes, we will. Wait!" Tara looked serious. "I see visions of where more of the men are right now."

"Where?" Jessie asks with excitement!

"Two of his men are drinking and fooling around five blocks from here at the local bar. Let's go and get them." The Stalkers take off once again flying in such a formation that looked like a flock of birds, leaving a cloud of dust behind. They circle the town which seemed like hour until the men are spotted.

"There they are. Look at them laughing; let's see if we can turn that laughter to fear."

"Good idea, Tara."

"That looks like one of the men who beat up my dad, I'm sure of it," says Tommy.

"The one with the large eyes does look familiar to me too."

"Alright guys, enough," Tara explains, "Jeremy and Jessie will attack. The rest of us will just watch." Finally, Jeremy kicks open the door and stares down the men with bright green eyes and fangs hanging from his mouth, meanwhile Jessie is hanging from the ceiling above with the same appearance as Jeremy. The men were clearly caught off guard, they didn't see them coming.

One of them said, "Hey, who are you kids? Get the heck out of here. Go and find some kids your own age. And why are you all dressed up, it's not Halloween!"

"We came to kill you." Jessie still in position as she spoke.

"What did you say? Do you two kids want to die, huh? Let me get this straight, did you say you came to kill me and my friend?"

"Look, I got three guns on me. I am not in the mood to play games with the two of you. How old are you? Fifteen or so and you want to kill us?" The men laughed so hard; the Stalkers were becoming annoyed.

"Now, kids, you had your fun. Now go on before we get mad. Now get out of here and don't mess with grown men."

"My name is Jeremy and she is Jessie. We are the Riverside Stalkers."

"Riverside Stalkers? What the heck is that a rock band or something?"

"You two kids are so funny. Hey, Augee, these kids are funny, aren't they? How do you think she's able to hold on to the ceiling like that, you must admit these kids have talent."

The men, still laughing, said, "Yeah, but they better go away. We got places to go now."

"As we told you, we are the Riverside Stalkers and we are vampires. We have come to get you two because you work for Mr. Mendoza. You two do great evil here in Riverside and you must pay."

"I had enough of this. Vampires. You two are crazy. that's enough of this, I'm going to beat the heck of out you two. You have been warned!" Jessie leaps down onto the bar directly in front of one of the men. He tries to hit Jessie with a beer bottle but misses several times.

"How did you two move so quickly? I can't hit you." He then pulled out his pistol and began to shoot Jessie, but she never flinched.

"Shoot some more, Augee."

"They won't die. Why don't you fall? Die! Die!"

"I'm out of bullets huh?"

"Now you men will die." Jessie grabbed one of the men around the collar and pulled him close to her face so their eyes would meet. Her eyes are glowing full force; the man is screaming that his eyes are on fire.

"Aah, aaah, help! Aaaah! Please it hurt so much." But Jessie's eyes never stopped glowing. In a few minutes, the man limp body fell over and she then let him go; she knew he was dead. Jeremy quick speed caught the other man at the back exit. He pulled him back in and began to choke him with all his strength, all you could hear was gurgling sounds from the man's mouth. He then put his hand right through his chest and ripped his heart out with one quick move.

"They are dead, Jessie. I pulled his heart out."

"Yeah, you really let him have it."

"I think you broke his back too, Jeremy. We should have not killed them so quickly."

"We should have made them suffer some more for all of their evil."

"No, Jessie, we did what we set out to do, remember we are the Stalkers."

"Good job, Jeremy and Jessie, we eliminated more of Mr. Mendoza's men tonight."

"Yeah, we sure did Tara. Just in this one night, we have killed most of Mr. Mendoza's men."

"Are we through for tonight, Tara? Are there more victims to get tonight?"

"Yes. I see a vision of one of Mr. Mendoza's men bullying an old lady. We are going there at once, but I want Erick to kill him. Let's go." The Stalkers once again fly away in the dark skies over the town of Riverside.

Chapter 22

The Stalkers find the old lady's house with Tara's guidance, and land in the backyard unnoticed; they could see through the rear window Mendoza's man harassing the poor woman. He's shoving her and shouting, "I know you know something."

She's crying and pleading. "I tell you I don't know anything, mister, please go! Leave my house."

"You better not be lying. We are going to find out who's killing our men."

Before the man finished his last word, Erick appeared out of nowhere, the man asked, "Who are you?" The Stalker remained silent glaring at the man with bright green eyes. "Why won't you answer me, kid? Let me get my knife maybe you might start talking then, and what's wrong with your eyes?" Erick still doesn't utter a word, but instead he grabs the man by his neck, raises him from the ground and leaves his shoes behind. At that time, the man manages to say, "Who, who are you," shaking uncontrollably. "Aaah, oh no! I'm sorry! Don't, don't!"

Erick speaks, "You are an evil man. You like to harass old ladies I see?" Just at that moment, you could hear a snap, Erick broke his neck.

Erick assured the old woman she was now safe and returned to his friends. Tara said to her friends, "We're going to call it a night. We will finish the rest of Mr. Mendoza's men tomorrow. We will bring him to his knees."

"Alright, Tara, are we really going after evil Mr. Mendoza?"

"Yes, we will and finish him off, Erick. Our families will be in more danger than before, I foresee Mr. Mendoza really turning on everyone in town." Emily was so afraid now than ever before.

"He is going to go crazy."

"But Tara, if all one hundred of his men are dead, then how could he become more dangerous?"

"Well, Erick, because Mr. Mendoza is going to bring more men to Riverside to kill the town people. I don't know exactly how he will do, but it's going to be really bad. We must get ready for the real battle to come." Tara had a concerned look on her face, she also was wondering if her friends were up for the battle with the most dangerous man that ever walked the streets of Riverside. Tara went on to say, "Our vampire powers are going to be tested so be prepared for what is about to come."

Chapter 23

"What is this? Last night, all of my men were slaughtered. Who could do this to my men?" Mr. Mendoza felt defeated, but couldn't let his men know how he felt.

"Their hearts were torn out of their bodies, their backs snapped, necks broken, and arms torn off. This isn't human. A normal person isn't capable of doing this. Almost all of my men are dead. Who could this be? Devil is dead, he was the most powerful one, I have twelve men left from over one hundred. Does anybody in this town know who my enemy is? Who is coming after me? Almost all of my men are dead. What are you? Who are you?" Mendoza is expressing his thoughts out loud. "I'm nervous. I'm scared. I got an invisible enemy. Look what they did to Devil. This isn't normal! This isn't normal at all. I'm mad as hell! I will burn this whole town down! I'm going to destroy everything in sight! My last twelve men are going to set this whole town on fire tonight! Tomorrow people better talk and tell me who my enemy is! Yes, they will talk!"

Chapter 24

Jeremy tells his friends he needs to check on his parents, he flies away and reaches his parent's house. His dad says, "Jeremy, my son, your mother and I never see much of you anymore, what's wrong?"

"Nothing's wrong, Dad, it's all good. There is nothing to worry about."

"I know you are ashamed of me, son, but don't run away from me. I'm just afraid of Mr. Mendoza because I got to protect you and your mother, Jeremy. Forgive me for being a coward, son."

"You are not a coward, I'm proud of you; very proud. I'm just hanging out with my friends. I'm not staying away from you."

Jeremy knew at that time he had to go to his room and avoid more conversations with his parents, they could not know his secret.

Meanwhile back at Riverside Lake House, Tara tells the rest of the Stalkers she too needed to leave, she hadn't seen her mom since yesterday. As soon as she arrived, her mom said, "Tara, you are always going out at night. Are you doing something illegal?"

"No, Mom, I'm not doing anything wrong. I'm just hanging out with friends. I came home to check on you, I know I was wrong staying away for so long, at that time Tara sensed something was wrong, a glimpse of fire appeared in her thoughts. I have to go, I'll see you soon." With lightning speed, she arrives back to the Lake House to tell the Stalkers they had another mission ahead.

"What's going on, Tara, you look irritated."

"I am, Tommy. Mendoza and his men are at it again." The Stalkers take off.

When the group get to town, you could hear the people shouting, "Town's on fire! Town's on fire! Riverside's burning, the town's burning."

"Look, Tara, Mr. Mendoza's sending a message, by burning the town we have to do something and quick," says Tommy. "There are those twelve men of his. Tara, look at them."

Mendoza's men had the people shaking and crying. One little old lady was on her knees praying, she could hear in the distance.

"Somebody better talk or we are going to burn your houses down so talk!"

"Who is killing our men? Last chance to name names, people of Riverside!"

"Tara, all of the townsfolk are staying inside. They are scared. They are afraid."

"Listen Stalkers, we are going to kill these creeps now."

"I could kill them within a minute by myself, but I want us to do this together. I want them to fear us." Tara's eyes began to glow these are the last of Mr. Mendoza's men that's on his payroll.

"But Tara, Mr. Mendoza is just going to go get more men."

"Emily, why do you seem afraid? Do you not trust your own power?"

"I don't know why I'm like this, Tara, I wish I had more courage." Emily felt ashamed.

Tara went on to say, "Well, we will kill them also, he can keep getting more and more men he then will realize he can't win.

Mr. Mendoza's time is running out. He doesn't have long before I will kill him. Now, let's go together and kill these twelve flunkies. Don't allow them to breathe an extra minute." The Stalkers were hovering above in the dark sky, Tara looked at them and they knew it was time to attack. Their eyes were all glowing a bright green that lit up the entire sky and town where the men were. One by one, the stalkers attacked. The men didn't have a chance all you could hear was, "Oh! Help! Please don't. No! No!"

"We did it; all twelve of them are dead." Tara was relieved. Jeremy, Erick, Tommy, Jessie, Emily, let's put out these fires."

With warp speed, each one the Stalkers put out the fire at different sections of town. Tara praised her friends; she told them that they did a good job. Emily was still acting nervous and asked Tara if anyone in town will tell what they saw. Tara told her to rest assure that their memories will be wiped away; she had the power to make that happen. She went on and said, "Stalkers, our mission is to save Riverside. I'm sure the people of Riverside would like to give us a medal for what we are doing, if they remembered our battle is far from over. We must be prepared for what is about to come."

"What's about to come, Tara, do you know?"

"Emily! Emily! Not again, stop worrying," she went on to say, "I can't put my finger on it right now, my visions are unclear. However, I know it is very bad. We've done our work tonight. We must go home to prepare."

Chapter 25

Mendoza and his son were at his place when someone tipped him off that his men were dead, and the town was saved from the fire.

"My town was burning. Who stopped it from burning? All of my men are dead." He is furious; veins are popping out from his temples.

"Who has done this? Who could this be? Why don't they come out and face me! I can't believe all of them are dead. They were tough. This isn't normal."

"Aw, Dad, I will have your back. We will get more men. We are going to continue to fight. We will crush them, we are Mendoza's we will win, and won't be defeated!"

"I know you have my back. Augee, you are a good son, but something's not right, this is bigger than us, I must find out who or what this is! We the Mendoza's are up against something that isn't normal. Devil was my best man and even he got destroyed. We are in trouble. If we get another one hundred men, I still think we will lose, son. I got to go bigger. I am going to the top."

"How could you go bigger with more men, Dad?"

Mendoza went on to describe how the men were killed in disbelief.

"Their hearts were pulled out, throats were torn out, and bodies broken in half." The people in town are not talking, so I will have to find out myself, what I am up against.

"Dad, let's get more men and I know they will find out who is doing this."

"I don't know, Augee. These killings are not normal. I just don't know."

"I promise. I promise we will find out who is responsible. We are going to kill whoever it is that's going against us."

"Okay, Augee. I will make a call and bring you another hundred men, but they better get our enemies quickly. I got a bad feeling about this."

"We will get them, Dad. They are as good as dead."

Chapter 26

The next day, Jeremy arrived at the Riverside Lake House first, waiting for the others to arrive, the teens loved hanging out there enjoying their summer vacation.

"Hey, Jeremy, where is your friend Tara?" He didn't know someone was following him; it was that annoying boy that had a crush on Tara, named Eddie.

"Come on Jeremy, does Tara have a boyfriend? Come on hook me up with her."

"No, Tara doesn't have a boyfriend, Eddie."

"Well let me get with her, man. She is the prettiest girl in school. No girl can turn me down. Not Eddie Banes. I am the man, Jeremy."

"No, Eddie. I know she doesn't want a boyfriend. She is too busy."

"She's not that busy if she's friends with you, Erick, Tommy, Jessie and that nerdy girl Emily."

Jeremy was now angry and says, "Eddie Banes, you can get Tara. She is not interested."

Jeremy was trying to remain calm but felt his temper rise, he knew what would happen if he didn't calm himself at once. Eddie said, "Jeremy, why are your eyes glowing? Where did you get those contacts?" Jeremy turned around to hide his face from the annoying boy, he couldn't let their secret be revealed.

"I don't know what you are talking about," Eddie said, forget it.

"That's alright. I will do it myself. She won't turn me down."

Eddie leaves the Lake House and heads to Tara's neighborhood hoping to run into her and he does.

"Hey, Tara, I want to talk to you. I want to ask you something, will you go out with me, how about it, Tara?"

"How about what, Eddie Banes?"

"Go out with me. You know, be my girl. I'm real cool and I drive a fast car. All the other girls want to go out with me. I'm the stuff; I'm the dude, Tara. "Come on, you know you want to, Tara. I want to date you because you are pretty."

"Forget it, Eddie Banes. I'm just not interested. I got to go."

"Come on you got to like me too? No girl can resist me, Tara."

"Well, this girl can. I just don't want to go out with you, Eddie."

"You are going to go out with me and you are going to be my girl. You hear me. I want you and there is nothing that you can do about it."

Eddie grabs Tara's arms and pulls her close to him.

"Eddie Banes, take your hands off me now."

"I will take my hands off of you when I feel like it."

"Eddie, I'm giving you one last warning. Get your hands off me."

She feels her strength getting stronger, she breaks away from Eddie and lifts him from the ground.

"Ouch! Put me down, Tara, my nose is going to bleed. Please put me down! I'm sorry, I'm sorry, Tara. I won't bother you anymore. I'm sorry, Tara. Please put me down."

"I told you I am not interested, but you continue to pressure me. Don't ever look at me again, you hear, Eddie? The bright green light is beaming from Tara's eyes, Eddie is now in shock, and doesn't comment on what he sees, he only could say I'm sorry. It will never happen again. I promise."

"I better not see or hear from you pressuring any more girls, you understand, Eddie?"

"Never again, Tara, I got it. Never again."

Tara drops Eddie, she paralyzes him and went on to say, "If it happens again, I just won't pick you up, I will break your back. Get out of here." When she took her powers off Eddie, he ran so fast he stumbled along the way. In the meantime, Jeremy decides to go to Tara's neighborhood to see if she was okay. When he sees Tara, she tells him all about the incident.

Jeremy, that Eddie Banes is so full of himself. I never saw a boy run so fast.

"Wow Tara, you probably made Eddie Banes set a world record for running."

"Yeah, I won't ever have to worry about him again. Jeremy, we got to have a meeting. Something is coming to our town."

Chapter 27

Tara and Jeremy head back to the Lake House to meet the rest of the Stalker, she tells them more trouble is heading their way.

"Like what, Tara?" Tommy asks. "More trouble, more men are coming to Riverside?"

"My visions see Mendoza bringing more men to Riverside."

"We're ready, Tara. All of us are ready to kill these men too."

"We will fight together. We will unleash a fireball of destruction on these evil men."

"Is everybody ready?"

"Yes, we can't wait." The Stalkers agreed. "We are ready to move with a power that these men have never seen."

"That's right. They are going against the Riverside Stalkers."

"Tara, you have many powers we don't have. One is your visions."

"Emily, my visions come from what I see through my mind, not with my eyes."

Meanwhile, Augee arrived at his home.

"Dad, I have one hundred men, the toughest I could find. They are at the warehouse ready for our orders. We are going to send these men out on the street looking and ready to kill." Mendoza looked very irritated.

Jeremy and Tara joined the rest of the group at the Lake House. She knew she had to really get her friends mentally ready for what was about to go down. She noticed Erick was not there, she asked the others if they knew where he was. The Stalkers didn't respond.

A few minutes went by then. Erick shows up and said, "Tara, there are a lot of vehicles arriving in town with Augee Mendoza leading them."

"I know where those men are going, friends. The visions from my mind say that they are going to the warehouse on North Street now."

"They must be setting up a plan to attack the town."

"No, Erick, they are awaiting orders from Mr. Mendoza. My visions also tell me Augee Mendoza is at the warehouse as well. Stalkers, we are going to attack that warehouse now. They are not going to know what hit them."

Once again, the group gathers in a formation like a flock of birds. The earth began to shake so fiercely, nearby trees and boats were destroyed because of the power they created together during their take off.

The Stalkers arrived at the warehouse ready for a battle. Their powerful landing alerted the men that they have arrived because of the rumbled and wind that followed them during their landing.

"So, you're the one who's killing my dad's men?" Augee demanded an answer. "What and who the hell, do you kids think you are?"

"We are the Riverside Stalkers and we are vampires. All of you that's here with Augee Mendoza won't leave this warehouse alive."

"So, you kids are the ones that killed our men and you are vampires?" The men followed orders and began to shoot their guns at them.

"Kill them, shoot all of those bastards."

Boom! Boom! Boom! Boom! "They won't die. We're shooting them and they won't die." All the men looked puzzled, and ran into the warehouse.

Tara yelled to her friends and said, "Jeremy, Jessie, Tommy, Erick and Emily, time to lock them in this building."

"Tara, we got all the doors of this warehouse locked. What's next?" Emily asked.

"Move aside, guys, I don't need any of your help I will single handily tear this building down and kill everyone inside." Tara's eyes began to turn bright green, and her breathing became intensified, as she began twirling around as if she were a powerful tornado, destroying everything in her path and the warehouse as well, the strength and power she showed was extraordinary.

"Done! This warehouse is destroyed. They're all dead."

"Those men made this trip for nothing. Augee Mendoza should have never wanted to be like his father. Now he is dead and his father is next."

"Let's leave this place now our work here is over," Jessie went on to say, "Tara, we are powerful, but you have powers that even a vampire shouldn't have. You destroyed that warehouse in a matter of minutes."

"This is why I am the leader, Jessie, because I believed in the lantern first."

"Mr. Mendoza won't give up. We will still have to battle him."

"Tara sees through her visions he will be hard to destroy but assures the stalkers they won't give up until he is defeated. She tells Emily not to worry.

"Riverside won't be free, our parents won't be free until he's stopped!"

The Stalkers went their separate ways.

Chapter 28

Mr. Mendoza was told about what happened at the warehouse and that all his men and his son was dead.

"My son! My son! My men, they are all dead. Who did this? How could this be?" He began thinking to himself.

"What is the power that I'm up against? My son is dead. What are you? Where are you?"

"I must get help. That's what I will do. I've got to get help. Who can help me? This isn't normal, I need help. I must think who can help me. Who can help me? I'm so tired. I'm not thinking straight. Who are you? I've got to get it together. Leave me alone. I will find you! You killed my son! You are not human, but I will get you somehow! You won't get me? Beebee Mendoza! Never! I can't be defeated! I'm the boss in Riverside forever! I need sleep. I need some doggone sleep. Let me sleep somebody. I got to get it together. I'm losing my mind. I'm losing my mind. My son is dead. I will get my revenge on whoever you are! I'm mad! I'm so damn mad, I'm going to get somebody! Listen to me. Beebee Mendoza doesn't run from nobody! I'm not afraid of you. I will do anything to get you! I will get you, my enemy!" Mendoza snapped out of his deep thoughts and began drinking.

"I got my bottle of gin; this is what I need to help me sleep; my bottle of gin. I'm going to drink this whole bottle." He is laying on an old couch talking to himself and slurring his words, he hears someone say get up.

"My boy is dead. Why should I get up? Why should I do anything anymore?" Mendoza staggered across the room and got another bottle of liquor and shouted, "Revenge! Revenge! I need more, I need to get drunk. Somebody's after me! I need to get drunk. I need help to track down these killers if it's the last thing I do, I will get my revenge! My power is slipping away. This isn't normal, someone is stripping me of my power." Mendoza is drunk and crying uncontrollably. "My bottle of gin will tell me what to do. I own this town! I will always own this town and everybody in it! Me! Beebee Mendoza! Revenge! I will get revenge for my son!" Mendoza passes out cold.

Chapter 29

"Tara, you are always gone. I know you don't like that I'm going to give in to date Mr. Mendoza. Is this the reason as to why you are gone from the house so much?" She was disgusted to hear that news from her mom.

"Tell me, I'm your mother. I feel you drifting away from me." Tara knew she couldn't tell her mother the real reason she was hardly around.

"I've been just hanging out with my friends. You know, Jessie, Jeremy, Erick, Tommy, and Emily. We are very close. I just like hanging out with them."

"Tara, I don't believe that. I really feel like you are keeping something from me." Tara tried to change the subject by asking her mom about her day but that didn't work when she began to bring up the idea about she just might have to go out with Mendoza. She also said, "People are going around town saying someone is killing his men, hopefully Mendoza is too busy trying to find out who it is that's out to get him and destroying his men, and perhaps he has forgotten about me."

Tara had a good feeling inside when she heard her mom express that and knew the town people were somewhat relieved if they are talking about it.

"Tara if I give into Mendoza, will you be ashamed of me?"

Her mother held her head down while she spoke.

"I'll never been ashamed of you, Mother, never. I know you will be going out with him for us and you would feel there is no way out."

"I will do anything for you, Tara. You are still my baby. I have no idea what Mendoza will do to me and it doesn't matter, when I saw the way he looked at you and said how beautiful you were, I knew I had to give in to him."

"Mother, don't worry. You don't have to worry anymore, whoever is going after Mendoza's men will defeat him as well, I'm convinced."

"Defeat Mendoza, Tara? Words going around town that he's in trouble. But, to defeat Mendoza, impossible." Tara's mom looked sad and hopeless.

"Mother, nothing is impossible. Mr. Mendoza will be stopped. He will never hurt anyone anymore."

"Wow, Tara, you almost make me believe what you say is true. Why do you say these things?"

"I just have faith. We got to have faith. If we don't have faith, we have nothing."

"Ah, teaching your mom some wisdom huh? I'm being taught by my 16-year-old daughter. I love you, Tara. I will do anything for you." She smiles and gives her daughter a hug.

"I don't want you to stay away because you are ashamed of me."

"Mom, for the last time, I'm not. I know Mr. Mendoza owns everything and everyone in Riverside and you are afraid like everyone else." She broke down and began to cry. Tara grabbed her mother before she reached the ground, but the grip wasn't strong enough to keep her in her arms, she couldn't let her mom know the real strength she possessed, so she eased her down to the floor. And they both continued to weep.

"I know you were protecting me. I know you had no choice and you felt you had to do it. I'm very proud of you don't ever think that I stayed away from the house because of you. I love you, Mom."

"I'm so happy to hear that, I don't want you to think, I am a bad and weak person." Tara held her mom's head up with both hands and said, "Look at me! I don't want you to fear Mr. Mendoza ever again because his days of ruling Riverside are coming to an end."

Chapter 30

Meanwhile back at Erick's house, while still in bed Erick hears his dad weeping, he runs down the stairs to see what the problem was. He asked his father why he was crying. He says, "I just feel so bad about being bullied by Mendoza."

"Stop crying, Daddy. There is nothing that you can change about what happened in front of me."

"I just didn't want you to see me be weak and helpless, Erick."

"It's not your fault. Mr. Mendoza is a very powerful man. He owns everybody and everything in Riverside and you didn't know what to do. Don't be so down on yourself. I got an idea one day soon we will go fishing, okay?" Erick was hoping that would cheer his father up and it did.

"Alright, son, that sounds good; we will go fishing." His father was now smiling. "Erick, I just want to say that you are a good son. I'm glad I am your father."

Later on, that morning, the Stalkers meet up to discuss what they're next mission would be. Tara's visions were now clearer than ever she knew what she had to do was almost unthinkable and if the others would agree and follow her lead.

"Why the sad face, Tara? We almost got Mr. Mendoza defeated. We have destroyed his men."

Tara answered her friend and said, "I had to look at the fear in my mother's face thinking and worrying about what Mendoza would do next."

"Yeah, me too, Tara." Erick responded, "My father still felt ashamed of getting smacked around in front of me. The look in his eyes I won't ever forget."

"All of us in Riverside have witnessed our parents being abused by Mr. Mendoza. We all have been victims by his cruelty." Jeremy was pacing back and forth as he spoke, clearing with a look of concern of his face.

"You're right, Jeremy. He bullied and cheated our parents out of their hard-earned wages and made jokes out of us. He made my older brother do flips down the street while he laughed at him. He is truly evil," Jessie tells the group, then she began to cry.

Mr. Mendoza's reign has affected people's lives so bad that our parents have not recovered, nor have the town's people; to feel helpless is like a disease. "I hope we can give hope back to the town of Riverside." Tara's eyes began to glow as they did when she showed uncomfortable emotions.

Chapter 31

Mr. Mendoza woke up feeling anxious and irritated, hoping everything that happened was merely a dream.

"Ah, a new morning. The whole town's probably laughing at me, but they won't any longer. I don't know who is after me, but I know who can tell me. Oh boy, how come I didn't think of this in the first place? I know what to do. I'm going to go to Zelda the witch. She is my special weapon. Ha, ha, crazy Zelda. The witch will help me. Ha, ha, Zelda will know."

Mendoza gets dressed in a hurry, not knowing he put on two different shoes. When he arrives at Zelda's Fortune, he started shouting, "Zelda, Zelda, are you here, Zelda?" It's me mister. Zelda, I need a favor from you. I need your help."

"I figured you come calling." The old woman grinned from ear to ear with missing and cracked teeth.

"I heard about your trouble in town. Word gets around."

"Yeah, that crystal ball of yours is your information, Zelda. That is your real power."

"Now, Beebee Mendoza, I have lots of powers, that's how I know who you are and your name." Mendoza was wondering if she could help him, he felt like his world was crumbling down right before his eyes.

"I'm here because I'm having trouble. Somebody is out to get me. Someone wants to take all of my money and power. I have an enemy."

"I need you to stop them. They killed all my men! I need you to use your powers to find a way to kill whoever this is trying to destroy me."

"Did I hear you correct? Kill them, Beebee Mendoza? You want me to do your dirty work for you?"

"Yes, this is what you do, Zelda. You are a witch and you put spells on people. This is why I'm here. I want you to find out within twenty-four hours. Because the way all my men were killed, this isn't normal. So, work your powers, you hear?"

"I'll do my best Beebee Mendoza but first you must pay my fee."

"Fee! I'm Beebee Mendoza! I don't pay any fee!"

"Well then, I can't help you." The old woman looked annoyed.

"Just because all of my men are dead doesn't mean I can't call up an army."

"Yeah, but it won't help you know who is behind all of this, now will it?"

"Alright witch, what is your fee?" Zelda could hardly spit the words out of the price she had in her mind, knowing Mendoza was desperate.

"It will be five thousand dollars and a bag of peanuts."

"What? Five thousand dollars? Are you crazy?" Mendoza slams his hand down on the table and says, "You greedy old witch, that's too much."

"Well, I can't help you if you can't pay."

Mendoza grabs the woman's around her throat and says, "Look, I can kill you, witch, you know this."

She broke loose from his grip and shouted, "Yeah, but killing me won't help you find your enemy, will it?"

"Yeah, you won't be any good to me dead, so I will let you live, and I will pay your five thousand dollars and your bag of peanuts."

"Make sure you have the money in hundreds, fifties, twenties, tens and dollar bills. That's how I like it. The woman insisted."

"I'll do that." Mendoza turned up his nose and said, "What you need to do is clean this shack out and get some air freshener, this place stinks, your dirty messy place smells like shit. And another thing. You should brush your yellow crooked teeth and wash your ass."

The old woman didn't seem to mind the cruel insults, Mendoza tells her she better make sure she finds out who his enemy is and that the information better be right. "Remember, twenty-four hours." Mendoza leaves.

Chapter 32

Tara calls for a meeting with her friends, they all arrive at Riverside Lake House, anxious to hear what their friend had in mind.

We have wiped out Mr. Mendoza's men. Now we have to wait for him to act against us. Tara's visions are letting her know he has inquired help from some kind of force. She went on to tell her friends, "Mr. Mendoza is plotting to find out who we are and he will act against us. We are not going to wait."

"Waiting will be allowing him to control us. We became vampires to liberate Riverside. So, listen up everyone, we needed to free our people, our families." Tara wanted to cry but couldn't, she then expresses to her friends, that Mendoza was making her mom date him.

"My mother should not have to become Mr. Mendoza's whore. All I have is my mother. She works hard and she tries to provide the best she can for me, yet this evil man wants to take advantage of her. I will kill Mr. Mendoza!" Tara eyes were glowing again, brighter than ever, then she said, "He will be destroyed and never come back, Mendoza will never come back! I will see to it that his death will be a death to remember. Being vampires is the only way of saving our families," Tara assured her friends.

"We all thought you were crazy when you found the magic lantern. It was a miracle." Jessie was twirling around and around with excitement.

"Jessie's right. That was a miracle that came into our lives. We didn't believe you at first, Tara, but it was all true."

"Guys, I believe it was a reason as to why I saw the magic lantern. I believe this miracle was meant to happen. I believe it was meant to do good for the people of Riverside."

"Tara, you are so wise. It was meant for you specially to find the magic lantern. You are the leader for us all. The magic lantern gave you much more powers than the rest of us vampires."

"I'm grateful for your comments, Emily, but our power is to fight for the helpless. Helpless is the state of no hope. That is what kills the soul, and we will prevent that from ever occurring again."

"Tara, you were always smart, but you've never talked like that before. I think the magic lantern made you smarter. It gave you brain powers also."

"I do find myself saying and thinking on matters that I didn't do before, Emily. We are all different now, friends, this comes with being the Riverside Stalkers. We are all faster than the speed of sound." Tara tells her friends when she woke up this morning, she felt different and was wondering if they felt it too.

"I find myself with no feeling of sadness that is all gone now."

"I do to," Tommy confessed, "having powers like this makes you feel in charge, in control, and bigger than life."

"Others use to laugh at my glasses, my loafer shoes and the fact that I had no friends." Emily expresses herself with confidence.

"Now that I am a Riverside Stalker, I feel important and strong. I feel like the entire world belongs to me and this feels great."

"Emily, we all feel like you, but our purpose is to rid the fear that lies in the minds of the town's folks of Riverside. Never shall the weak be struck in a position of uselessness again."

"We will fight for all. For everyone, we the Riverside Stalkers have a purpose that is bigger than ourselves." Tara instructs the Stalkers to recite a passage.

"Justice for all, helplessness is buried forever."

"Now let's get some training because our biggest battle is yet to come."

Chapter 33

"Do you see what Mr. Mendoza will do next, Tara?" Emily asked nervously hoping her friend had the answer.

"We all know he is coming with two hundred men. Isn't that right, Tara?"

"I'm not sure, friends, but an inhuman force is about to come. Mr. Mendoza is seeking help from the dark side. We will need to use all of our powers to combat this bad spirit. We can't show any signs of weakness or show our enemies we are helpless." Tara gathers the Stalkers and made them show her one by one what each of their powers will allow them to do.

"Emily, concentrate. Use the powers of your fingertips to make that tree move fast."

"I did it! I did it, Tara! It worked! My powers are stronger than I thought." Emily repeated over and over all I have to do is concentrate.

"Tara, this training session is a great idea." Tara instructed the Stalkers one at a time to demonstrate what they could do and they did.

"Jeremy, use more of your mind control in battle and your flips."

"Good idea, Tara, my flips really threw them off balance."

"Tommy, use more of your speed with sharper hand speed. Jessie, use more of your breath of wind powers to cause chaos and allow you to attack quicker with your kicks. Erick, use more speed with judo and more powers in every blow you give. If ever in battle, and you are at a disadvantage, as a last resort, use your vampire fangs and bite."

"Tara, this training session has made me realize that I have more powers than I thought."

"Me too, Jeremy, I didn't even know that my fingernails are weapons. My fingernails are better than knives and razors." The Stalkers were all proud of their powers and strength.

"Our powers are unlimited. We must use our imagination when we are going against a great foe." The leader goes on to say as she stares at a tree nearby, while a red beam came from her eyes.

"Look guys, look at that tree. See how it's burning. The flames from the burning tree could be seen from a mile away."

"Yeah, Tara, you can make fire come out of your eyes."

"I'm using my imagination to create the fire. When I open my mouth, I can create a tornado or windstorm." When Tara demonstrated to the gang what she could do, everyone grabbed onto trees to keep from blowing away. "Look again friends, bullets! I can make these bullets attack with deadly force, right from my mouth." Tara shows her friends all what she can do, the teens were amazed and silent as they looked on.

"My karate is second to none. My speed and strength is unmatched. I can throw the largest tree with one arm. I can knock down any tall building with ease."

"Wow, Tara! You have more powers than all of us. You are incredible."

"Yes friends, I do have more powers, but remember to always use your imagination."

"This was fun, Tara, really fun. I'm ready for anything."

Tara was wondering if her most intimidated friend could handle the battle that they were up against, she replied to Emily, "We have to be ready. Something fierce and powerful will be coming at us; a dark force. Mr. Mendoza is seeking help from the supernatural world. My visions tell me it will happen soon, guys."

"Do your visions see who or what it is, Tara?"

"Is it more men? Is Mr. Mendoza going to bring more men to kill us?" Jessie seemed very anxious while Tara tried to explain.

"No, Jessie, my visions tell me it is deeper. It comes from the supernatural world."

"Supernatural world? What could that be, Tara? What is coming to us?"

Tara looked at each of them while her eyes were glowing, they knew she was becoming frustrated with all the questions and said, "Guys, it will be a great challenge. We are well trained, but our minds must be ready as well like never before. We are on a mission. We must prevail for the people. We must use all of our vampire powers." The Stalkers all nodded in agreement.

"Tommy, use more of your speed with sharper hand speed. Jessie, use more of your breath of wind powers to cause chaos and allow you to attack quicker with your kicks. Erick, use more speed with judo and more powers in every blow you give. If ever in battle, and you are at a disadvantage, as a last resort, use your vampire fangs and bite."

"Tara, this training session has made me realize that I have more powers than I thought."

"Me too, Jeremy, I didn't even know that my fingernails are weapons. My fingernails are better than knives and razors." The Stalkers were all proud of their powers and strength.

"Our powers are unlimited. We must use our imagination when we are going against a great foe." The leader goes on to say as she stares at a tree nearby, while a red beam came from her eyes.

"Look guys, look at that tree. See how it's burning. The flames from the burning tree could be seen from a mile away."

"Yeah, Tara, you can make fire come out of your eyes."

"I'm using my imagination to create the fire. When I open my mouth, I can create a tornado or windstorm." When Tara demonstrated to the gang what she could do, everyone grabbed onto trees to keep from blowing away. "Look again friends, bullets! I can make these bullets attack with deadly force, right from my mouth." Tara shows her friends all what she can do, the teens were amazed and silent as they looked on.

"My karate is second to none. My speed and strength is unmatched. I can throw the largest tree with one arm. I can knock down any tall building with ease."

"Wow, Tara! You have more powers than all of us. You are incredible."

"Yes friends, I do have more powers, but remember to always use your imagination."

"This was fun, Tara, really fun. I'm ready for anything."

Tara was wondering if her most intimidated friend could handle the battle that they were up against, she replied to Emily, "We have to be ready. Something fierce and powerful will be coming at us; a dark force. Mr. Mendoza is seeking help from the supernatural world. My visions tell me it will happen soon, guys."

"Do your visions see who or what it is, Tara?"

"Is it more men? Is Mr. Mendoza going to bring more men to kill us?" Jessie seemed very anxious while Tara tried to explain.

"No, Jessie, my visions tell me it is deeper. It comes from the supernatural world."

"Supernatural world? What could that be, Tara? What is coming to us?"

Tara looked at each of them while her eyes were glowing, they knew she was becoming frustrated with all the questions and said, "Guys, it will be a great challenge. We are well trained, but our minds must be ready as well like never before. We are on a mission. We must prevail for the people. We must use all of our vampire powers." The Stalkers all nodded in agreement.

Chapter 34

Mendoza pays the old woman another visit and reminds her it's been twenty-four hours. He kicks the door open and yells, "Zelda, when are you going to get my help? I'm anxiously waiting."

The old woman says to the impatient grumpy man, "Just watch, Beebee Mendoza, just watch what I can do." The old woman began to rub on the glass ball and says, "Agubocka, agubocka, I'm calling upon you. Come forth my Orkin, Orkin come forth! Come forth and avenge, avenge Beebee Mendoza's enemies. Come and kill them. Kill those who are after him. Orkin… Orkin…kill! Orkin, Orkin kill!" Mendoza was becoming irritated by the woman's commands.

"Crazy old woman, who is Orkin? Who is Orkin, old lady?"

"Orkin, is your best friend. He is a monster. He is half bear, half zombie and ten feet tall. He can't be killed, the Orkin can't be killed. He will kill your enemies, Beebee Mendoza, he will help you."

"Well, where is this Orkin, Zelda, where is he?" Mendoza demanded an answer.

"He comes from the ground. I got seeds from hell. I lay these seeds down and call him and he will come. Allawa,

Allawa, almighty Orkin come and fight this man's battles. The Orkin will terrorize the town of Riverside tonight."

Mendoza yells, "Are you sure he will avenge for me, crazy Zelda. Huh?"

"He will, Mendoza. Your enemies won't be able to defeat him, never! The Orkin has two heads. He is all of bear and zombie. A thousand men could not do what he will do for you Beebee Mendoza."

"You still don't know who my enemies are, Zelda." She continues to look into her crystal ball and answers Mendoza to say.

"Your enemies are powerful, and you did right to come to me." He started pacing the floor, every now and then hitting the walls.

"I just want them dead. That's all, so I can go back and rule my town, Riverside."

"You willc, Beebee Mendoza, I promise you that." The old woman tried to sound convincing, so Mendoza could stop hitting the walls, the building wasn't in the best of shape.

"I haven't slept in a long time. I need peace, and to remain king of Riverside."

"You will always be king of Riverside, Beebee Mendoza. The Orkin will come alive tonight. It will scare everyone in town."

"Now Zelda, I don't want this Orkin to kill all the people in town because if it does, I won't have anyone to pay me their dues and taxes." Mendoza went on to tell the old witch how his business operated.

"The people of Riverside have to pay me taxes when they get a job because I own all the businesses. I own everything in town. They have to pay me property taxes and sales taxes. They have to pay me taxes if they want to keep their jobs. Nobody in Riverside is free from me, Zelda. I'm the boss! I'm the big man! I own those small people of Riverside! Those regular folks are small people! I am the one who they look up to! I'm the guy who has money! The little people are nothing! You are only important when you have money and power! The more money you have, the more superior you are. The regular people are nothing!" Mendoza wouldn't stop with his rants. "Hard working people are nobodies, nevertheless I need them. I need them to make me richer. I love money. Money is all that matters. I don't care about the people of Riverside, but I do need them to pay me their money. I don't care if your Orkin kill my enemies, Zelda, but I need the townsfolk alive. So you make sure that monster doesn't kill the people, I need them. I only want my enemies killed."

The old woman rolled her eyes and said under her breath, "How many times his old ass is going to repeat the same thing over and over." Mendoza thought he heard the woman say something and demanded she say it again. She remained silent, knowing what might happen if she made him angry. He started his rants again.

"I want my enemies to die tonight, Zelda. I want this man, whom ever he may be, I want him to feel pain when he dies at the hands of your Orkin."

"Zelda, when Orkin kills my enemy, I will give you your five thousand dollars and bag of peanuts."

"You have a deal, Beebee Mendoza, you have a deal."

"I'm out of here." The woman was pleased to hear him say he was leaving that she began to grin exposing those horrible teeth. "My goodness that crazy witch's shack stinks so badly, and so does she." He was fanning the air as he was leaving and said, "I see why she doesn't have a man. No man can kiss her with those yellow teeth. She sure comes in handy. She is going to find my enemies and her black magic will kill them. It's good to know an evil crazy witch. My goodness, that smell should be against the law," he continues to walk away and says, "now I will be calm. My enemy will go down."

Chapter 35

Mendoza was thinking to himself, *I got to make sure all angles are covered just in case that witch didn't keep her end of the bargain.* He had to get word around and warn the people of Riverside. After pondering on it for what seemed like hours, he came up with a solution to his problems, Mendoza began to talk out loud while pacing the floor.

"I will have my people at the media who work for me to report on television and radio that something bad is going to happen in town real soon. I also got to have some of my people walk the streets with a bull horn warning them to lock their doors and stay inside their homes. I don't want the Orkin that crazy Zelda created kill my citizens, because I need their money. I can't have my townsfolk getting killed. I told that stinky old witch to just kill my enemy, that's all. I don't fully trust her. I didn't get rich by being stupid. I need these folks."

Chapter 36

Meanwhile back at Tara's house, her mother was doing a few chores while listening to the news and heard something was going to happen in town something very bad. She yells to her daughter who was upstairs, "Tara! Tara! Come down quick." She was shaking and very nervous. Tara makes it down the stairs like a bolt of lightning, Mom! Mom! What's wrong. Her mom responds with a shaky voice.

"Tara, there's a warning on television that all of us should stay inside tonight. If anybody is outside, they will be killed by a creature. I don't want you to go out with your friends tonight."

"Mother, everybody in town has heard these warnings. Mr. Mendoza has some men going around with bull horns warning all of us."

"I don't trust anything that evil man says, he doesn't care about any of us in this town. He also sounds as if he's going mad telling us a creature will kill anyone out on the streets tonight." Tara had to say that to her mom because she knew the real truth, her visions revealed everything that was about to happen.

"Tara, Mendoza is all on the radio everywhere giving that message."

"I also heard from my friend tonight that everybody in town is afraid. Since this warning has come from Mendoza, people believe him."

"That is why I need you to stay in tonight." Her mother still speaking with a shaky voice.

"Mom, don't be afraid, remember, Mr. Mendoza's power comes from fear and bullying. Don't give him anymore power."

"Well, dear, everyone in town knows that Mendoza's men are all getting killed by someone. Maybe he's trying to scare us all, but just in case I want you to stay in and not go out with your friends. I don't know what I would do if something happened to you. You are all I've got. I can't lose you." Her mom began to weep and hugs her daughter tight.

"Mom, you will never lose me, I promise. Don't worry, it will all work out right."

Chapter 37

Tara leaves the house to meets up with her friends. When she arrived at the Riverside Lake House, everyone was present. She couldn't help but to call out their names one at a time.

"Jeremy, Erick, Jessie, Tommy, Emily, have you all heard about the town warning from Mr. Mendoza?"

"Yeah, Tara, we all heard. What do you believe? Tell us, Tara, what do you see? Emily's curiosity was impressive to Tara."

"My visions tell me that something bad is coming and we must be ready."

"Mr. Mendoza is responsible for something far worse than we can imagine."

"We all must meet together outside of town to plan our attack on this evil omen."

Meanwhile back at the old witch's shack, Tara's visions allow her to hear the woman recite the spell that will bring the Orkin to life. The ugly smelly old lady rubs the crystal ball and says, "It's dark; it's night of all night of darkness. You Orkin on my orders come alive and go kill Beebee Mendoza's enemies. Go to Riverside! Come alive! OOWA!!! OOWA!!! OOWA!!!" All of a sudden, a ten-foot-tall beast appears out of nowhere, his hairy body, large paws, sharps claws, red eyes and two enormous heads that shook the witch's shack as he walked toward her.

"There you are, Orkin, you came alive. Go and hit the streets of Riverside. Kill Beebee Mendoza's enemies. I love your growl Orkin. OOWA! OOWA! That's a great sound. You are born to kill. Go do what you are ordered to do! I'm your master. Me, Zelda! Zelda, I'm great! No witch is better than me. There will be no other like me! Orkin, I've created you. Make me proud!!! You will kill anything in sight, nothing can stop you. Go kill, so I can get my five thousand dollars and my bag of peanuts. You're a ten-foot tall, two-headed bear, and zombie. Go find and kill Beebee Mendoza's enemies. Now go!!!"

Chapter 38

Tara's mom continued to do her chores when she heard a loud noise coming from outside. When she went to the window to take a look, she saw an enormous creature approaching, he was so scary looking that the sight of it made her knees buckle. She began to scream.

"Help, help, the monster is coming. Help the monster is coming. Please someone help us! We are doomed, the monster is here!" She calls out to her daughter, "Tara, a monster!" Her daughter never answered. "Where is my daughter? I told her to stay inside. Where is she?" Tara's mom couldn't believe she left even thou she pleaded with her not to.

Back at Jeremy house, his dad had also heard about some type of monster that was going to destroy the entire town and everyone in it. He searched the entire house for his son but had no luck. He began to yell, "Where is Jeremy? The monster is here, please, son, come home please!" His dad fell to his knees and began to pray.

Meanwhile at Tommy's house, his dad was pacing the floor, calling out to his son, "Tommy, where are you? The creature is in town." Tommy never answered his dad, then he began to worry.

Meanwhile at Emily's house, her parents were frantic when they heard the news that a monster was roaming around town. They too began calling out to their daughter.

"Emily, where are you? Where are you?" Emily never answered.

"Stalkers, my visions tell me that Mr. Mendoza's creature is in town. It is terrifying everyone it sees and roaming the streets looking for we, the Riverside Stalkers. He will have to fight to the finish if he wants to battle with us." Tara's visions are more enhanced than ever. She tells her friends, "We will strike and strike hard; we won't be defeated. Let's go and get him now. Let's fly. We will take off now. Let's go destroy this monster." The Stalkers take off into the sky with speed faster than a bolt of lightning, their formation in the sky always looked like a flock of birds, except one of them seemed to have fallen behind breaking up the beautiful pattern they once had. It was poor Emily; she seemed to have run out of energy or enthusiasm and confessed to her leader.

"Tara, my flying is limited. I don't know if I can fly all the way in town." The Stalkers were instructed to land by their leader.

"Emily, you can fly, you must believe in your powers. Your flying abilities will work as long as you believe."

"Maybe you're right, Tara, but why can't I keep up."

"Maybe you are second guessing yourself so stop it right now." Again Tara reminds her she not only has to use her strength but also her mind. The Stalkers looks at Emily as if she were a nuisance.

"Emily, Tara is right. If you don't believe in yourself, then your powers are useless, we all can fly with ease including you." Tara thanked Jessie for trying to help Emily gain more confidence in herself again and gave her a big smile.

"Like what," Tara said, "our powers are unlimited. We just got to believe."

"Erick, what do you mean you just got to believe?"

"What I said, Emily, stop doubting yourself."

Tara gets frustrated and yells, "Enough, this talking is over, let's go to town and fight that monster this will be a tough battle; we need to be mentally prepared as well as physically."

"Tara, your powers are superior to ours. I believe and feel safe being under your leadership." The Stalkers all agreed and formed a circle holding hands.

"Let's go and save Riverside. The monster seeks us, so it's our duty to keep the people of Riverside safe we have to fight it."

"Stalkers, let's go and destroy this creature."

"Tara, look next to the library it's the monster; it's huge and has two heads."

"Stalkers, I need all of you to go on the attack now. I will join in last. I will put a merciful attack to support you all with all of my powers. Now attack!" Jeremy leaps across the street with great speed right above the creature's head.

"Jeremy, the monster is shooting nails and smoke out of its mouth. Look out! He thanks his friend for warning him with a nod. Jeremy tried to sneak an attack from the back, but it seemed like the monster had eyes behind its back.

"Wow, the monster just hit me with its big claw." Jeremy had a trickle of blood run down the side of his face, but that didn't stop him, he continued to fight. He yelled out to Tommy, "His mouth has a laser beam and I just got hit! It hurts a lot!" The creature's attack was more than what they bargained for. He kept shooting fire from its mouth without hesitation. The Stalkers had to dodge the fire as if they were being used like target practice.

Tara shouts, "Jessie, use all of your speed you have to keep moving. Emily will use her wind to see if she can blow him down. Jeremy, Erick, and I, really need you, we need powers from all angles if we are going to defeat this creature."

"I got hit again from the monster's right claw." Jeremy stumbles almost going to the ground, he catches himself and swears, and tells his leader.

"The monster's laser beam from his mouth hurt me it burns really bad, Tara. I've hit it with everything I have he won't go down! He won't go down! What will we do?" Tommy saw that his friend was in trouble, so he pounced on the monster like a flash of light. He took his knife out stabbed the monster several times but nothing happened. Then he dug his nails into the eye of one of the heads of the large beast again nothing, the beast was not affected. The teen's eyes began to glow as he became more and more angry his fangs came out. He quickly grabbed one of the heads and bit the creature. The creature flung the teen across the street again it was not affected. Tara looked down at her friend with pity, he began to speak.

"Tara, my sharp knife and sword like nails aren't hurting it. I've punched the monster with full force, used karate kicks, bitten it with my vampire fangs and still nothing hurts it." Tara calls on Jessie to help.

"Jessie, help Tommy." She began blowing a strong wind from her mouth, again nothing happened.

She tells her leader. "It's not moving the monster is not moving like it should."

Tara tells the Stalkers, "I'm in now you guys, I'm in on the fight." The creature hit Tara with a beam that was so hot, she screamed out in pain. She regained her composer and tried karate kicks, judo chops, then blew fire from her mouth on the monster again nothing fazed it. Tara flies back across the street where the other Stalkers stood and tells them, "The two-headed monster should be hurt, but it continues to resist. I even opened my mouth and allowed fire to strike it, also I used the beams from my eyes to penetrate and burn his, but nothing happened. I was trying to blind him. Look, everyone, the monster is moving slowly."

Emily shouts with excitement, "I think he's hurt, but yet he resists. So what's next, Tara, we will still fight!" Jeremy leaves the group to battle with the creature again. He open-handed slaps it with the force of a bulldozer, the beast seemed a little stunned, then punches the teen as hard as he could in his chest, Jeremy falls and yells.

"I've been hit! I'm hurt, but I will keep on fighting. I will use the palm of my hand again to hit him as hard as I can." He tells the group, they knew he had the most power in his hands, Jeremy felt his claw around his neck, then the monster let out the most excruciating sound imaginable.

The teen broke free and began to run back to his friends. "We are going to retreat; we'll have to come back." Tara insists, "Let's go now." The Stalkers take off the same as they always did leaving a cloud of dust behind, trees swaying, branches breaking from them.

"Tara, look the monster is jumping up and down. Is it because we are leaving?" The Stalkers could see him from above as they were flying away. They finally reached their destination, on top of a three-layered mountain as the large bright moon was shining in the background. "Tara, why are we running away from the monster?"

"I don't run from anyone, Jeremy; we are here on the mountain to regroup."

"The monster thinks he won, Tara, did he win?"

"No, he didn't win, Jeremy. We hurt him very badly, but it's hard to beat."

"I'm going back to fight him by myself and I promise I will kill that beast." Tara eyes began to glow, everyone knew she was frustrated.

"You are going back to fight him by yourself? Oh no, Tara, you must have us with you to fight that enormous creature." Emily seemed worried trying to talk her leader out of the decision she made.

"No, I am the leader and my decision has been made. I will return alone and do battle with him. I will destroy the monster."

"But Tara, we are the Riverside Stalkers; we are six, not one." Erick challenges his leader.

"Erick, there are six of us, but the magical lantern gave me the greatest power and I can defeat him by myself."

"Tara, we didn't defeat the monster. He got the best of all of us." Jeremy also had some concerns.

"I know, Jeremy, but I know what I did wrong and I know what I can do. I didn't concentrate with the power of belief."

"Power of belief, what are you talking about, Tara?"

"Listen all of you, my powers are so great, I didn't believe in the use of all of them. The creature doesn't have a clue of what I am going to do with him."

"But Tara, you even opened your mouth and released fire and that did not kill him," Jeremy reminded her.

"The monster won't touch me this time. My speed will be too great for him. My speed will be much faster. The creature won't be able to keep up. He won't be able to see me."

"Well, Tara, we see that your mind is all made up, but we want to watch the battle from afar." The Stalkers knew their leader was not going to let them help her, so they remained quiet.

"Watch, my friends, I will destroy him."

Chapter 39

Meanwhile back in town, the old witch pays Mr. Mendoza a visit to inform him about what happened between the Orkin and his enemies, but before she had a chance to tell him, he had already begun to talk.

"I heard there was a great battle down by the old library building doggone it and I missed it."

The old woman said, "Yes, that's why I'm here, the Orkin beat up your enemies. He got the best of them. I watched it from my crystal ball. The Orkin cannot be defeated."

Mr. Mendoza said, "I wish I knew that the battle was going on, Zelda. How come you didn't tell me when the battle was coming?"

"I didn't know, Beebee Mendoza, I just felt it."

"You're not making any sense." Mendoza was becoming frustrated.

"Just felt it? You are a crazy witch. Well, you said he beat my enemy up, but he didn't kill him. Who is my enemy, you crazy stinky witch, who is he?"

"Your enemy is my enemies," the witch explains.

"What does that mean? I need them dead. Are you going to tell me or not, you crazy witch?"

"Your enemies you don't know, and it doesn't matter. The Orkin will kill them eventually."

"Well, make sure they are dead, do your job, witch."

"And you make sure when your enemies are killed, you pay me my five thousand dollars and bag of peanuts, Beebee Mendoza."

"Crazy witch, at least you created that monster for me so I should be in good shape. I will continue to own Riverside. Mendoza began to grin from ear to ear talking to himself, and occasionally hitting the wall."

"I am the boss! I'm the only boss of Riverside! I'll never be defeated! Life is so good, I'm still King. Me, Beebee Mendoza! And for you, you stinky old witch, the job better get done and I mean done right!"

"Calling me names don't hurt my feelings as long as you Beebee Mendoza bring me my money and my bag of peanuts. I know I stink. So what? That don't hurt my feelings, I like my smell." The witch leaves Mendoza place mumbling to herself.

"When the Orkin kills his enemies, he better bring me my money. If doesn't pay me my money, I will turn the Orkin on him."

Chapter 40

Meanwhile back at the beautiful hills of Riverside, all you could see where the shadows from the bright moon reflect over the lake and the teens. Tara calls out to her friends, "Jeremy, Erick, Jessie, Tommy and Emily, the visions of my mind tells me this evil witch had created this creature."

"Where is this witch, Tara?" Jessie asked.

"She lives in a shack down by the river at the other end of town."

"We must go now and kill this witch; she is responsible for all the madness."

"Let's go and confront her and teach her a lesson." The teens fly away leaving a path of destruction through the forest trees as they follow their leader to their destination, soon they arrive at the old witch's shack, the howling of the wind alerts the woman that something or someone was on her property, she peeps out the window and showed little fear, Tara demanded the witch to come out.

"You old witch, we know you are inside, come out and face us."

The woman responded, "What do you kids want with me? I don't know you. What do you want?"

"We are the Riverside Stalkers, and we know that you created that monster to kill us." Tara's visions were much clearer than they ever been before, she could see the witch with that old ball of glass creating that horrible creature that was now terrorizing them.

"Yeah, I created the Orkin and yes, I know you are Beebee Mendoza's enemies."

"So you are going to be destroyed by the creature."

"Why did you create him? Tell us at once, witch." Tara's eyes were now glowing with anger and hate.

"I did it because Beebee Mendoza needed my help, he said someone were killing off his men, and If I would help him, he would pay me money and a bag of peanuts."

"For some money and a bag of peanuts? Wow. Are you kidding, witch?" Jeremy asked.

"No, Jeremy, the witch is right I can see the whole thing in my visions," Tara tells her, "money and a bag of peanuts, that won't ever happen."

"What are you talking about? Won't I get paid? I will get paid."

"No, you won't, we are vampires and I'm the leader, Tara. I am going to kill your Orkin."

"Vampires? I knew it. I sensed you all have supernatural powers, but you will never defeat the Orkin."

"Witch, I am going after your Orkin to kill him, but first I will make sure you won't be able to create another creature."

"My Orkin has already beaten all of you and you can't beat him."

"You, Zelda the witch will not be able to harm another person of Riverside again." The glow from Tara's eyes became more pronounced as the witch continued to irritate her.

"So, you know my name huh, dear girl?"

Tara frown at her and responds, "Yes, I know your name and you are evil." The witch goes on to say, "I know your powers are far greater than any I've come upon, because I have never seen anyone eyes glow like your does but I'm afraid you still can't beat my Orkin." By this time, Tara was now facing the witch.

"Never, dear girl, will you or your vampire friends defeat him."

"You are a foolish witch, doing Mr. Mendoza's evil work for money and a stupid bag of peanuts. We will make it that you can't ever use your arms again. You will never talk again and finally never walk again." Tara looked the witch straight into her eyes until she began to holler, the woman was begging for mercy but Tara ignored her cries, the witch eye sockets were as hollow as the opening in the ground, with black smoke coming from them, but she was still alive.

Emily shouts, "What else are you going to do with her? Aren't you going to kill her?"

"Yes, Emily!"

"We are going to put her in a pit down by the lumber yard."

From the instructions from their leader, the teens rushed inside, grabbed the witch and forcefully removed her from the smelly old shack, she was screaming and hollering, "Your kids will pay for this you will all be destroyed." Tara tells the witch to shut up and that she will die slowly. They all flew away with the old woman, with her still shouting profanities. The Stalkers spotted the pit from above, Jeremy and Emily each had one of the old woman arms. Tara tells them to let her go, you could see her screaming and pointing as she descended toward her final destination. In a matter of seconds, the witch was undetected.

"We have just put the evil Zelda in the bottomless pit. Nobody will find her, Tara."

"That's right, Emily, my visions tells me she will never be found and is still alive. I want her to suffer and die a very slow death." After the Stalkers finished off the witch, they flew back to the mountain to discuss their next plan, Tara tells them she alone will battle the creature, the teens listened to hear, but the looks on their faces were looks of disappointment.

"Tara, we don't understand why you insist on fighting this Orkin alone. We can kill it together, Tara, all for one," Tommy explains!

"I foresee that all five of you will have a lot of trouble trying to fight this Orkin."

"But, Tara, you could not defeat this Orkin either."

"Do you also foresee yourself having trouble as well?" Tara had an uncomfortable look on her face and starts to explain.

"I know what I did wrong. My powers were never an issue, it was my concentration."

"Once I concentrate. It will be impossible for anything to defend against me."

"We are the Riverside Stalkers; we are the defenders of the powerless, and the destroyers of all enemies."

"Your powers are greater than even you are aware, but my powers are unlimited. Nothing or no one will defeat me, do you hear me," Tara was now shouting at her friends, "I have made my decision, so don't question me," she began to rant more.

"My powers are far greater than anyone can understand. This Orkin's greatly evil. It is incumbent that I, the leader of the Riverside Stalkers, should defeat him. I'm the only one."

"But being the Riverside Stalkers, I still believe we should fight the Orkin together." Tommy was still not convinced she should battle the creature alone.

"The decision has been made, as I said before, I will defeat him."

"Besides, I don't want to risk any of you being killed. I am the chosen one, I have the power that is unmatched. Now when the time comes, we will find the Orkin. The creature only roams the street at night. In a matter of a few days, the Orkin will be down the road near the Pike building." Tara's visions were on high alert, she knew exactly the day and where the creature would be.

"Can we be there with you, Tara? We want to be there when you do battle with this Orkin." Tommy again was concerned about his friend being alone.

Tara answered, "Yes, if you insist, but you can't interfere with my battle. As your leader, your confidence in me is still a test of my greatness."

"Tara, regardless of what happens between you and this Orkin creature, we the Riverside Stalkers will kill Mr. Mendoza together right."

She answered her friend and said, "Yes, this is what all of this is all about. We will finish him forever."

The teens all nodded their heads in agreement with their leader.

Chapter 41

Tommy confessed to the group about what Mendoza was doing to his uncle and cousin, he began to explain.

"Tara, my Uncle Harry has a ten-year-old son who is in a wheelchair. He was born with an infliction. Uncle Harry wants to leave Riverside, but he is afraid that Mr. Mendoza would kill him. As we all know, my Uncle Harry and all our fathers who work in Riverside have to pay Mr. Mendoza taxes for having a job. My Uncle Harry knows that he still owes Mr. Mendoza for his job and he told him if he leaves Riverside, he would hunt him down and kill him. My Uncle Harry's son, who is crippled, feels helpless, and afraid, he can't sleep at night and neither does my uncle, the boy cries constantly. My uncle told me he wants to sneak out of town, but he is afraid that Mendoza will catch and kill him and his family. The people in our town shouldn't have to live in constant fear. They and our parents are close to out of their minds."

"Tommy, we will go and talk to your Uncle Harry at once." Tommy and Tara tell the other Stalkers they were going to town to speak to his uncle and will return later, both teens take off like two soaring eagles through the mountains and trees breaking off branches leaving destruction behind as they flew. Finally, they reach the uncle's house.

"Tara, this is my Uncle Harry and his family. This is his son, Teddy. He has been in this wheelchair all of his life." Tommy tells his uncle to explain to Tara what was going on but seemed a little reluctant.

"Talk to her uncle, she is my friend. Don't be afraid." His uncle responded and said, "Well I guess."

"A friend of Tommy's is a friend of ours." He began to talk. "As you can see, Tara, I am so afraid, I want to leave Riverside, but I can't because I still owe taxes for the job, I have at this tire factory."

"Mr. Mendoza has raised taxes on everyone who works at the tire factory, and I got behind. As you see, I have a sick son, I had to take time off work to see after him and I just got behind paying on my taxes. Now on top of everything else theirs this creature that is roaming our streets, I'm so afraid to leave the house to work, Tara, I feel backed up against a wall but if I find the courage to leave, Mr. Mendoza will find me and my family and kill us all. I am so scared I don't know what to do."

"This creature is keeping us in our homes. My nephew told me to talk to you. Why I don't know, you are just a teenaged girl."

Tommy butted in and said, "Uncle, Tara is a person you would not want to know, but she can be very helpful." Tara began to tell his uncle about how they met and that she had more friends, and they were all the same age and maybe he would relax more and began to trust her.

She went on to say, "Tommy is a good friend of mine and whatever I can do to help him I will, in fact the rest of my friends, Emily, Erick, Jessie and Jeremy feel the same way as I do, we are very close." Tommy mumbled under his breath and said in more ways than you will ever know, and then smiled.

"This creature will not roam the streets of Riverside for long I promise. Uncle Harry, your worries will end soon."

"Young lady, I hope that you are so right. I'm about to have a nervous breakdown." Tara noticed the boy didn't say not one word while she was there.

"Your son, Teddy, doesn't talk much huh?"

"No, he doesn't talk much at all. He's been like this all of his life." She felt so sorry for Tommy's family, if it was the last thing, she did is to make sure the people of Riverside will be at peace again. Tommy and Tara leave the uncle's house.

On the way out, Tommy was weeping and says to his friend, "My aunt and uncle do the best that they can."

"Tara, I am so worried about them. I'm also worried about my parents and the others as well."

"Everybody in Riverside is on edge and are half-crazy Tara. This includes the parents of Jeremy, Erick, Jessie and Emily."

"My mom is very worried as well, Tommy, they all are."

"I must go and see her at once." Again, Tara's visions reveal to her that her mom is very upset.

"I will go with you, Tara." Tara and Tommy arrive at her house, and immediately her mother yells out!

"Tara! Tara! I've been so worried, I told you not to leave the house. I haven't been to work because I'm afraid of this monster and you go out to be with your friends." Her mother is so furious that she doesn't realize that she is hitting the walls and stomping her feet.

"Don't you kids ever obey your parents? There is a monster out there at night with two heads ready to kill. Please stay inside."

"Mom, we all will be together and not put ourselves in danger. Go and get your rest, everything will be just fine." She tries to assure her mother, but it didn't work.

"Tara, it's getting dark. The creature will be out very soon."

"No, Mom, I know where and when he will be out."

She pulls Tommy into another room and tells him, "My mom is very upset. I've never seen her like that before."

"Everybody's upset, Tara, everybody." Tara tells her mother she had to go and not to worry but it was useless, her mother was pulling on her as she tried to leave, but Tara broke loose from her, she cried out, "Please! Please don't go." Tara continued to leave as Tommy followed and said to him.

Chapter 42

"We will go now." Tara and Tommy flies away from the house and never looked back, they didn't want to see Tara's mom begging and crying just in case she came outside looking for them. They arrived back on the mountain with the others, after they told the others what was happening in town Tara felt something come over her, it was another vision, she knew it was time, time for her powers to really be challenged, she expressed to her friends, I will go and meet up with the Orkin and end this at once. Remember Stalkers don't try to interfere with the battle.

"I can hear the Orkin now. I can hear his growl." Tara's vision was now telling her the creature was near, she thought he was coming in a few days, but he was on his way now.

She tells the others he was a few miles away, Erick responds to say, "Wow, Tara, the Orkin is miles away. You can hear ten miles away."

"No, Erick, I can hear twenty miles away and I can hear the creature now, I am ready. I am going to fly at a speed that is faster than the speed of sound. I hope you guys can keep up." The teens gathered as they always did and take off in their formation, weaving in and out through mountains and trees until they reached the open black and grey sky. Tara spots the creature and directs the Stalkers to stand by.

The Orkin was destroying buildings, and she knew perhaps she could catch him off guard. Tara attacked the creature with all that she had, first she struck him in the eye with a swift blow the creature stumbled but remained erect she then opened her mouth and let out an enormous stream of fire hoping the creature would burn. Tara continued shooting fire from all angles, even the bright green glow from her eyes became fire as well. Tara continued to open her mouth and what seemed like missiles that was coming out connected the creature but didn't faze it. Tara began to spin like a whirlwind in the dry dessert, she shouts out in a loud voice take the wind and take the fire that I give to you, die creature! Die, the monster began to growl as the flames pierced its body, again another growl, the Orkin began throwing flames at the girl from a distance. The Stalkers yells.

"Watch out, Tara, the Orkin is throwing fire too." The creature was swinging and punching and throwing blows at her. Tara was still twirling around so fast nothing touched her. Emily shouts out with excitement.

"Look, you guys, he can't touch her, she's too fast."

Tara opens her eyes real wide, sending laser beams of explosives hitting the Orkin. Then another beam of explosives followed. The Orkin was now hurt. Tara then got close enough to the creature reached into his chest and ripped his heart out, the large monster fell to the ground and then there was silence.

"The Orkin is dead. Hurrah, Tara has killed the Orkin. The evil monster is dead." The teens were all celebrating, jumping around cheering and laughing.

"Tara, you did it! You did it! You killed the evil witch's monster. You were unbelievable. You were unreal, never seen such speed and power. There is nothing you can't do, nothing! Wow!"

"Now we see why the magic lantern chose you. You are fantastic. Never before have we seen such greatness and power. Each Stalker congratulated their leader one by one."

"The Orkin is dead. What's next, Tara?" they all asked.

She responded and said, "What's next? Mr. Mendoza is next." The Stalkers flew back to the mountains, where they could discuss their next plan of attack on Mendoza. It's about time; we want him so bad, we can taste him. Jessie says in an angry voice. Tara tells them, "Riverside Stalkers, you can't kill Mr. Mendoza."

"Why, Tara! Why can't we kill Mr. Mendoza? What are you talking about?"

"I will do it I have a special death for Mr. Mendoza."

"He is going to have a death like no other death. Our town has been tortured by this brute for far too long." Jeremy jumped up and started expressing himself now trembling and angry.

"Our parents are slaves for this evil man. Tara, we have stopped his paid helpers, that evil old witch, and that two-headed monster. He can't be allowed to go on with this. I want to tear his throat out."

"No, Jeremy, I want to tear his heart out of his body."

"He doesn't have a heart," Jeremy reminds her. Jessie was pacing saying what she wanted to do to him over and over again.

Tommy says to her, "No, Jessie, I want to tear all of his body parts up and strangle him, you took the words right out of my mouth." Erick then said what he wanted to do also, Tommy tells him to get in line.

Tara stands up and shouts, "Enough! I know you all want a piece of him, but as I said, Mr. Mendoza is mine."

"Tara, we know that you are our leader, but you are leaving us out. We are the Riverside Stalkers. It's not just you, we want to kill him as well." Jeremy looked very frustrated as he spoke.

"My death for Mr. Mendoza is much greater than what any of you can do by killing him. He will die the way all evil men should die. So, I must kill him. I'm the one who can do what must be done."

"I fully trust Tara, Jeremy, she's our leader. She knows best." Emily grabs Tara's hand and smiles at her and Tara smiles back at Emily, she then said, "We all put our trust in you, Tara, with full confidence."

"We will always trust in you, always." The Stalkers apologize to their leader for complaining earlier and agreed with Emily.

"I'm grateful for all of your trust in me my friends. My journey is to free this town and free our people, it's upon us at this moment." Tara's is now having another vision; she shares it with the others.

"I can see where Mr. Mendoza is, he is back at that old witch Zelda's shack looking for her.

"But he will never find her, right? She's been taken care of, right Tara." Emily changed her mood drastically by the mentioning of Mendoza's name.

"Yes, she has, her death was well deserved. Lets' go and meet up with Mr. Mendoza. He is going to be in for a full surprise."

Chapter 43

The Stalkers again take off from the mountain top with full speed. This time they were not in their usual formation, it seemed as though everyone was trying to race one another. When they arrived, Tara was already there. She startled the old man so bad that he jumped when Tara appeared, then she asked.

"Mr. Mendoza, are you looking for Zelda the witch?" By then, each of the Stalkers landed one by one, then he asked in a trembling voice.

"Who are you? What do you kids want? I don't have time for you."

"What? How can you kids float up in the air like that?"

"Is this real? Am I dreaming? What's going on?" Mendoza was now shaking.

"You won't be able to talk to Zelda, Mr. Mendoza, because she's dead. You see, we the Riverside Stalkers, have killed all of your men. We also killed everybody that was helping you."

"It's you! It's your kids that are my enemy! You kids!"
"Yes, Mr. Mendoza, we are vampires. A different breed of vampire we were created because of your evilness upon Riverside."

"Your rule has come to an end. You will never rule Riverside again."

"You! It's you that murdered my son! You killed my son!" Mendoza was shaking his fist, his fear turned to anger.

"No, Mr. Mendoza, it was you who killed your son. You taught him to be evil like you, to be a bully like you and to be cold-hearted like you. Now you are going to die. You are going to die with a purpose." Tara eyes once again began to glow. He warned the teens and said,

"I got a gun; I'm going to use it! I'm not going down without a fight!"

"I'm no punk!" He began shooting at the kids, and said, "I'm shooting and you won't die, die, die, die you damn kids!"

"We told you, we are vampires and you should know no bullets can kill a vampire." Tara's eyes glowing even brighter.

"What do you want with me? What you want? Everybody wants something. You want me to believe you are vampires? Okay I will."

"No, I don't believe you are convinced even though we killed all your men and killed that evil witch and her two-headed monster that she sent to destroy us. We will show you," Tara demanded him to look Mr. Mendoza, "see us fly. Look at Emily throw your truck. She picked the old truck up as if it weighed only a pound and tossed it across the road. Now do you believe?" Mendoza eyes nearly popped out of his head and he began to beg and cooperate.

"Vampires! What's this world coming to? Even vampires want something. What do you need, blood? I can get you blood, all the blood you ever need. Come on, kids,

I will give you a blood bank. I will give you all the money you will ever need. Please, please, leave me alone. Give me a break."

"Did you give the people of Riverside a break, Mr. Mendoza? Why didn't you give them a break?"

"I gave the people of this town jobs and housing. I was good to these people."

Tara yelled, "Silence! I don't want to hear another word you have to say." She grabbed him by his head and made him look her into her glowing eyes so he could see all the pain and suffering he brought to the town's people.

He cried out, "Stop. I can't take it anymore, please I don't want to see it, I'm sorry!" Each time he tried to break free, Tara would make the glow from her eyes burn his.

She told him, "You cheated the people of Riverside. You abused them, you bullied them in front of their children. You bullied and abused our parents in our faces. You bullied my mom to go on a date with you. She begged you to leave her alone, but you wouldn't. The people of Riverside had to pay you an unfair amount of their money. You abused with such a force of evil. You, Mr. Mendoza, have been sentenced by the Riverside Stalkers to die. You are going to die, Mr. Mendoza. Your life will end." Mendoza's pants were wet and then there was a puddle of water under his feet.

"Oh no! Oh no! Come on, I'm sorry. You got to give me another chance. Please don't kill me."

"We all are not going to kill you, only me. Take you last breath because this breath of yours has ended." Tara started chanting over and over.

"I command you evil spirit to come out of this man."

"Tara, what are you doing? You supposed to kill him, not exorcise him."

"Yeah Tara, kill him." The Stalkers were all confused.

She says to her friends, "Guys relax, I am killing him. Just watch. I command all of you devils to release this man and to all come out of this man at once." Mendoza starts to wiggle his body uncontrollable.

"Look, Tara is doing a miracle. Look! Look! Look, snakes are coming out of him." The Stalkers were all shouting, we can't believe it.

"Snakes everywhere are coming out of Mr. Mendoza. Look at his eyes. They are rolling back into his head." Each time a snake would exit his body, it would make a loud howling noise. "Snakes are coming out of his nose, mouth and ears. And out of his stomach, everywhere out of his body." The howling noise was almost unbearable.

Now, Mr. Mendoza has fallen to the ground.

He has stopped breathing.

"Look Jeremy, Erick, Jessie, Tommy, and Emily."

Mr. Mendoza is breathing again, he's getting up. When he stood up, it was a bright light that reflected from his body; he also had a smile on his face that the teens never seen before, he clearly was a changed man.

"Bless you, bless you, dear Tara. I'm free, I'm free. I feel love, I feel love. I will learn to love everyone." He was sobbing and still expressing his feelings.

"I'm so happy, and I feel like a new person. I will help everyone. I will use all my money to help people. No more taxes."

"I will give to the poor; I will give to the sick and I will help sick children."

"I will do nothing but good deeds. I will give love to all and every day for the rest my life. I feel so happy. I have so much joy. I am alive to serve people forever." Mr. Mendoza ranted for over an hour about what he had in store for the people.

"Tara, what's going on?"

"Yeah, Tara, what is going on?"

"Tara, Mr. Mendoza was dead, now he is alive. What is going on?"

"My friends, what you have witnessed is amazing. I had killed Mr. Mendoza and I made him come alive as a new person."

"He is now a new man. I casted all the demons out of him so he could be free."

"Free to love, free to give love and kindness to all. The old Mr. Mendoza is gone, a new life is here. He is now free."

"Tara, is this what you meant when you said that you must kill him yourself."

"Yes, my friend, this is why I had to kill him myself."

Emily was so proud of Tara she began to weep. Mendoza was weeping as well, he said, "Thank you, dear Tara, for freeing me. Thank you for allowing me to love. There is no greater feeling than to love others. Mr. Mendoza, be on your way. You are free."

"I will forever be on my way to give love to all." The old man leaves the teens, looking back at them waving occasionally until they were out of his sight.

"That's it, Tara, it's over."

"Yes, Emily, it's over. Dry those tears. Mr. Mendoza is here to give love."

Out of nowhere Jessie spots a strange object, as she looked closer, she said, "Look, you guys. There is the magic lantern, how did it get here?"

The voice from the magic lantern had the Stalkers' attention; it said, "You the Riverside Stalkers, your mission has been completed. You have freed the people of Riverside. I only have one question for you. Do you wish to continue to be vampires?"

"What do you think, guys?" Tara asked her friends. She wanted them to make up their own minds.

Tommy reminds her and said, "You are the leader, Tara; your decision is final."

The magic lantern again speaks and ask. "Do I grant you the power to forever be vampires or return to normal teenagers as you were?"

Tara responds and says to the lantern, "Dear magic lantern, I wish, we wish to serve the helpless and the hopeless. Yes, we want to remain the Riverside Stalkers."

"Your wishes and desires have been granted."

The End